Larkspur Bungalow

Julie Meulemans

ISBN: 978-1-4834-2726-3 (sc)
ISBN: 978-1-4834-2725-6 (e)

Lulu Publishing Services rev. date: 3/4/2015

I dedicate *Larkspur Bungalow* to Steve and Kate.
Thank you for challenging me to find my voice.

Chapter 1

Meredith Delaney was born Meredith Singler. An unconventional Pacific Northwest beauty, tall and stately but known best for her thick blond curls. Meredith never considered herself pretty. She much preferred to be competitive in academics and athletics. She grew up in the West Hills of Portland, Oregon, the only child of a heart surgeon, who was well known for his impossibly demanding yet impressive techniques at Oregon Health and Science University. The teaching hospital, which sat atop the highest hill in town, was often referred to as "Pill Hill" by the locals. Although behind Dr. Singler's back, his students referred to it as "Pill Hell" due to his incredibly high standards. His kindhearted yet militant expectations of his only daughter were no different. He believed that a little pressure motivated those around him.

"The apple didn't fall far from the tree," her mother always said. Even as a child, Meredith was as driven as Dr. Singler, and she worked tirelessly to achieve success in every aspect of her life. On weekends, she and her father carved out time to run. They were equally competitive, often racing from their house to the hospital. Once they'd finished the five-mile ritual, they hung out in the park, chatting endlessly about everything from their beloved Portland Trail Blazers to the laundry list of colleges that Meredith longed to attend. She was wickedly smart, and prided herself on the impressive list of elite schools she had compiled over the years. At the top was Stanford, her father's alma mater, where he had easily finished first in his class. While he did not insist she follow in his footsteps, he was pleased to know that he had inspired his daughter to emulate his drive for academic success.

Dr. Singler had completed his four-year stint at the prestigious West Coast university thirty years before. He had gone on to the distinguished Harvard Medical School, where he ultimately had his pick of residencies upon graduation. It had been a surprise to many that he settled in quirky Portland, but he loved the energy of the Northwest and knew early on that he wanted to spend his years practicing medicine in a teaching hospital.

It was not too long after moving to Portland that Dr. Singler met and proposed to Meredith's mother, Grace. They had remained happily married, and now, to their disbelief, their daughter was preparing to graduate from high school. It seemed like it was just yesterday that they'd brought their baby girl home from the hospital.

For seventeen years they had savored their weekends, which they spent reading the *Oregonian* at their favorite Starbucks and walking hand in hand along the scenic Willamette River. When Meredith was small, she loved wedging herself between them, with the occasional alley-oop over a puddle left behind after an especially rainy morning. But their threesomes grew few and far between once the teenage years descended upon them. Saturday mornings no longer began at dawn. Like most teenagers, Meredith typically did not surface until at least noon, and then rushed out of the house with the gaggle of trusted girlfriends she had known since nursery school.

As her senior year in high school commenced, she knew she would need to whittle the list of colleges down in order to make her final decision. She was not at all concerned about being accepted, as she ranked second in her class and had received a nearly perfect score on the dreaded SAT. As Christmas neared, she announced that she had decided to attend Stanford in the fall. Both Dr. and Mrs. Singler were thrilled for Meredith, but Dr. Singler was especially moved, brushing a proud tear from his eye following his daughter's announcement. She had worked very hard and was deserving of the many accolades that came her way during her last year in high school—everything from academic achievement awards to a state championship trophy as part of the school's renowned track-and-field team. Yet Meredith continued to take it all in stride, accepting the honors humbly and with poise.

The final semester of her senior year flew by, and it was not long before they were making the road trip to sunny California, where Meredith would spend the next four years taking in everything college had to offer. She embraced her years at Stanford, and though she enjoyed the football games and parties, she always put her studies first. Graduating magna cum laude from one of the most reputable schools in the country afforded Meredith the job of her choice. Her father always hoped she would become a doctor, but that never interested Meredith. Deep down she was a creative soul, and she hoped to eventually incorporate her love for painting and writing into her career path.

As a graduation gift Meredith's parents took her to Europe for a month. They visited France, Italy, and Spain and ended the trip in Switzerland. While the sites of Paris were grand and the canals of Venice magical, Meredith's favorite part of the whirlwind vacation was traveling through the mountains of Switzerland. She would never forget taking the train through the narrow swath of trees, ultimately arriving in the quaint hamlet of Gruyère, where they enjoyed a decadent pot of fondue with a crusty loaf of freshly baked French bread in the tiny town square. It was the perfect trip, and she would always remember how special her parents made her feel.

Upon arriving home to Portland, Meredith's immediate task was to find a job and an apartment of her own, although her parents made it clear she was welcome to live with them as long as she needed. Secretly, they hoped she would stay indefinitely. Unlike many of their friends, they loved having their daughter at home; they felt like the years had passed too quickly. But they understood, and were proud of her independence.

Meredith submitted her résumé to many local companies and was pleased to have a number of interested employers invite her to interview right away. Her degree from Stanford was an asset, and it was even more impressive that she was nearly fluent in Spanish and French. Within three weeks, Meredith had four job offers. When all was said and done, Meredith, like her father, opted to accept a position that would help others while still allowing her to keep her hand in the field she loved. She proudly announced to her parents that she had decided to assume the role of copy editor at a small publishing company. They primarily handled unknown writers, which she saw as a way to support those who desperately wanted to be published yet lacked the resources or connections with the larger mainstream publishing houses. Meredith beamed as she animatedly pointed out that over the years, the small but formidable company had developed an excellent reputation for discovering fresh new writers, eventually propelling them to national and, in some cases, international success.

The first month flew by. Meredith could not wait to go to work each morning. She found a small studio in the Pearl District, situated over a French bakery, which made breakfast easy, as the heavenly waft of freshly baked croissants filled her apartment each day. For lunch she usually brown-bagged it. Her parents begged her to accept a small stipend each month, but Meredith refused. It was important to her that she exert her independence and not rely on her parents for support. On Saturdays she scoured the secondhand shops, filling her small flat in a way that rivaled any eclectic coffee table book from Anthropologie.

Meredith often met with longtime friends for cocktails, hashing out the events of the week, as well as the lack of potential suitors. They had all dated off and on, but none of them had experienced long-term relationships. They were too busy with their academic and professional goals, unintentionally relegating men to the back burner. Regardless, they enjoyed each other, and cherished the fact that most of them had decided to return to Portland after college.

As Thanksgiving drew near, Meredith took a well-deserved week off, opting to sleep in every morning and visit with out-of-town friends over coffee or wine. Naturally, she spent Thanksgiving Day with her parents, at their annual gathering of twenty longtime friends and colleagues, but she ducked out before dessert to meet a group of high school friends at Huber's Cafe. They had discovered the restaurant's decadent Spanish coffees on Meredith's twenty-first birthday, after which they had made Portland's famous watering hole their official gathering place.

As the week came to an end, Meredith began to feel antsy to get back to her desk. She was expecting a new book from a promising young author and could not wait to delve into the manuscript. As expected, Monday proved to be an exceptionally long day, and just as she was grabbing her coat, the phone buzzed. Though she was tempted to let the answering service take the call, she decided to pick up the phone at the last minute, and was surprised to hear the familiar voice on the other end of the line.

"Hey, Meredith, it's Chandler Harris. Happy holidays!"

Chandler was a friend from Stanford, with whom she'd had a cursory relationship confined mainly to the third floor of the campus's Green

Library. She'd met him during her final year as both dutifully engaged in epic study sessions, vowing to finish strong. They often took breaks together, filling up on coffee and bagels, banking on caffeine and carbs to get them through their last term. Chandler had been finishing up his law degree, always an ominous concept to Meredith. She simply could not imagine the tenacity required to practice law. But Chandler had great drive, undoubtedly seeking an eventual payout with his golden ticket from the prestigious Stanford Law School. He always made it abundantly clear that his idea of professional success included money and fame, two things that had never interested Meredith. But she did not fault him, and got a kick out of his ambition.

"Chandler, great to hear from you! How did you track me down?" Meredith knew Chandler had family in Portland and figured he was visiting for Thanksgiving.

"I just moved here last month. I am basically the assistant to the assistant at the U.S. Attorney's Office. The pay stinks, but if I play my cards right, it will be worth it in the long run. I called your parents' house, and your mom was nice enough to give me your work number."

"That's terrific, Chandler! Wow, a soon-to-be federal prosecutor. Where are you living?"

"I found a small apartment in Hawthorne. It's not bad. I jump on the MAX in the morning, and I'm at work in fifteen minutes. How about you?"

"I'm in the Pearl District. We should get together sometime." Meredith looked at her watch. She was getting more and more tired, and desperately wanted to go home and fall into bed. But she did not want to seem rude. Chandler was sweet, and she did not want him to think she was blowing him off.

"Actually, I know it's last minute, but I'm meeting a friend at the VQ in a few minutes and thought you might like to join us for a drink. I hear the martinis are the best in town."

Meredith paused, trying to quickly come up with an excuse.

"Come on, Mer. Just one drink."

She smiled. "Oh, all right! But just one drink, Chandler. I've had one of those days, but I really want to see you."

"Great, Mer. See you in a bit."

She stopped in the ladies' room, where she added a little lipstick while simultaneously releasing her mane that she characteristically twisted into a bun. She always pulled her hair out of her face when she worked so she could concentrate on reading manuscripts without her curls falling into her eyes.

As she entered the popular Veritable Quandary, or, as the locals called it, the VQ, she spotted Chandler immediately. He was standing at the bar, and waved as soon as they made eye contact.

"Hey Chandler, great to see you," she said, giving him a huge hug.

"Same here! Meredith Singler, I'd like you to meet my friend, Peter Delaney."

"Hi, Peter. Nice to meet you. Do you two work together?"

"Peter is an old family friend," said Chandler. "He's a hotshot associate at Bailey, Sanders, and Kensington."

"Far from it," Peter said, shaking hands with Meredith. He nervously took a swig of his IPA while quietly acknowledging that Meredith was even more beautiful than Chandler had let on. He figured that he was probably five years older, but that did not seem like a big age difference. After all, most of his friends were chasing women far younger than Meredith.

A booth opened up and they grabbed it, settling in and ordering a round of the famous VQ martinis. They were made to perfection: a little dirty, served up with three huge olives.

"So, tell us about your new job, Mer," Chandler said.

"Well, I've only been there for a few months, but I love it! In fact, I just started reading a new manuscript that I really think has the potential to be a best seller."

The three of them chatted easily until nearly midnight, promising to get together again soon. Meredith counted the evening a success as she walked the three blocks to the riverfront, where she could easily grab the streetcar to her loft in the Pearl. During the ten-minute ride, it occurred to her that she was going to regret that second martini in the morning.

Chapter 2

Tuesday morning arrived more quickly than Meredith had hoped, and she awoke wishing that she had passed on that last cocktail. However, she'd had a great time catching up with her old pal and meeting Peter. She thought Peter was very nice but had not really gotten to know him because he'd been a bit quiet. Maybe he's just one of those guys, she thought. It also occurred to her that maybe she had dominated the conversation. Regardless, she didn't have time to rehash the events of the evening because she was running late for work.

She dragged herself into the shower, already thinking about the manuscript that awaited her. An extra-tall cup of coffee and a plain baguette were all she could tolerate, while quickly making her way to the office. As she began working on her new assignment, she slowly started feeling better, managing to leave behind her queasy stomach.

At ten o'clock her phone rang. She reached for it while continuing to read. "This is Meredith."

"Hi, Meredith. It's Peter Delaney."

Meredith sat up in her chair as the manuscript slipped through her fingers and onto the floor. "Hi, Peter."

"I just wanted to tell you what a great time I had last night. I was wondering if you wanted to have lunch today?"

Meredith was initially caught off guard, but she salvaged the moment by accepting with the same breezy confidence she'd exhibited the night before. She may have seemed calm, cool, and collected, but she instantly had a pit in her stomach. After she hung up the phone, she dashed outside to get a breath of fresh air. Why was she so thrown by the phone call? She felt ridiculous. "It's one lunch," she mumbled to herself as she returned to her desk, where she thumbed aimlessly through the pages of the manuscript.

As noon drew near, Meredith looked forward to lunch with cautious anticipation. She decided to embrace the "win the day, don't worry about tomorrow" mantra that had always served her well. Just as she smiled at the personal reminder, her phone rang.

"Hey, Meredith. I'm about five minutes away."

"Great! I'll come down and meet you in front of my building."

Peter gave her a short hug, and she was pleased to learn that he had made reservations at Jake's. Meredith had enjoyed many family dinners there over the years, always ordering their famous clam chowder, which was served with a huge basket of fresh bread.

They walked up Stark Street, chatting effortlessly the whole way. Meredith was surprised to learn that Peter shared her love for art, and happily agreed to join him for the opening of the Matisse exhibit at the Portland Art Museum. At lunch, both Peter and Meredith ordered the chowder, talking endlessly about all sorts of subjects. It was a terrific lunch and both returned to their respective offices feeling satisfied and encouraged.

Because she had taken the prior week off, Meredith knew she would have to log some extra hours to make up for the unanswered emails and stacks of paperwork that had accumulated on her desk during her absence. The week flew by, and by Friday afternoon Meredith was pleased that she had been able to clear her inbox and respond to the pressing needs of her clients. Her plan was to have a quiet weekend, starting with a hot bath and a facial, her go-to ritual after a long week.

Just as she started up Oak Street toward her loft, she heard that familiar ping that indicated a new text had registered on her phone. She read the text while waiting for the light, and smiled when she saw that Peter wanted to get together over the weekend. She slipped her phone back into her bag, trying to think of something fun she and Peter could do.

As she rounded the corner, she looked up to find Peter standing in front of the red-brick building that she called home. He was so handsome, she thought, smiling there in his suit and tie. She could not believe that someone so attractive would be interested in her.

"Hi there," she said.

"I hope you don't think I'm stalking you, Mer."

It was the first time he had called her that, and she loved the way it sounded.

"Not at all," Meredith said, unlocking the front door.

"I was hoping you could join me for dinner tonight," Peter said. And he looked at her in a way that gave her a rush of excitement.

"Sure." She motioned for him to follow her up the five flights of stairs.

"Don't you have an elevator in this place?" Peter joked.

"I think it's the reason the rent is so affordable. Plus, it keeps me in shape!"

As they entered the loft, Meredith could tell by Peter's face that he was impressed with her clever sense of design.

"Did someone help you decorate your loft?"

"No. I'm obsessed with quirky stuff in secondhand shops. It never makes sense to me when people go out and spend ridiculous amounts of money on boring rooms of beige furniture when you can find unique stuff for way less at thrift shops. I just mish-mash it together and call it a day!"

"Where did you find the artwork?"

"Um, I did it," Meredith said, with a hint of an awkward apology.

"Meredith, this is really good! I'm totally impressed. Were you an art major or something?"

"No, just something I always dabbled in. I know my style is a little unconventional," she said, surveying the pieces that hung on the wall. "Which is why I never really wanted to take art classes. I guess I always thought I would be told I was doing it all wrong."

"I wouldn't change a thing. The huge martini is definitely my favorite," Peter said, pointing to the colorful painting over the fireplace.

Meredith smiled. After all, they had met over martinis at the VQ. She explained that the year before, while at a local art exhibit, she'd been inspired by a painting of a huge martini that was far out of her financial reach. So she replicated it on a canvas that she found on sale at a local art supply store. The finished product was far more abstract than the original, but it suited Meredith's eclectic sense of design. In fact, she had several friends who'd offered to buy it if she ever grew tired of it.

"So, where do you want to go?" Peter said.

"I could whip something up. I think I have a bottle of wine somewhere around here."

"Great! If it's not too much trouble," Peter said.

It didn't take long for Meredith to produce a simple but gourmet feast, which they enjoyed in front of her small fireplace. It was the perfect evening. Great food and a bottle of pinot noir from Meredith's favorite Oregon winery while the Portland rain poured down outside. It was not long before they realized it was well past midnight; they had been talking nonstop for hours.

"I really like you, Meredith," Peter whispered. He leaned over and kissed her. His hands found their way to Meredith's blouse, and he slowly pulled it from the pencil skirt that she had worn since early that morning. She did not fight it, even though in the back of her mind she was concerned that he would expect her to go further than she was comfortable.

"Peter, I think we should slow it down a bit." She didn't believe her own words as they fell from her lips.

"I am just so attracted to you, Meredith. But I don't want you to feel any pressure."

She loved that he was understanding, and felt she owed it to him to tell him exactly how inexperienced she was so he would not think it was lack of interest. Meredith had never felt this way, but she wanted to be wise and not move forward too quickly.

"I should probably tell you, um, well . . ."

"What is it, Meredith?"

"Ugh. This isn't easy," she said. "Okay, I'm just going to say it. I'm a virgin."

"What a relief," Peter said. "I thought you were trying to find a kind way to kick me to the curb!"

"I don't want to kick you anywhere, Peter," Meredith said with a smile. "I just need to move a little slower."

"Done!"

Clearly smitten, he kissed her softly, promising to call the next day for a proper date.

Chapter 3

Peter and Meredith began spending all their free time together, which made Meredith feel a little guilty. She had not made any effort to see her girlfriends in over a month, but she could not bear to spend her limited free time away from Peter. It had been almost two months since the couple first met, and they both knew they were soul mates.

On an especially stormy February day, Meredith was at her desk, so consumed by her work that she had unwittingly missed lunch.

"Hi, Peter," Meredith heard the receptionist say. Just as she looked up, Peter waltzed around the corner.

"Hey, what are you doing here?"

"I have a little surprise for you," he said with a very smug look on his face.

"What is it?"

"You'll just have to wait and see." And with that, he took her by the hand, escorting her from the office.

"While this is a lovely idea, Peter, I can't just leave the office in the middle of the day without telling anyone," Meredith chirped.

"Don't worry. I talked to your boss, and you're not expected back until tomorrow."

"Really, Peter?" Meredith said with the excitement of a child.

"Yep. Now follow me, and no more questions."

They walked up to Broadway and into the Benson. It was the oldest hotel in Portland, proudly known for accommodating every president since William Taft. Meredith had eaten countless Sunday brunches in its dining room and attended many formal events in the ballroom, but had never stayed the night.

"Are we having lunch here?" Meredith inquired.

"I told you, Mer. No more questions."

She gave him an eye roll, and giggled when he playfully wagged his finger at her. As they made their way across the lobby, she suspected this was going to be better than lunch. She secretly wished she had worn something else that day. She had a new outfit hanging in her closet that she was saving for a special occasion. This would have been a perfect opportunity.

Peter grabbed her hand, and just as he did she noticed a dignified gentleman carrying two key cards in one hand, a familiar bag in the other. It was her leather weekend bag.

"Hey, that's mine," Meredith said.

"No questions, remember?"

"Excuse me, but I think I have a right to know if you have been rummaging through my loft," she whispered to Peter in a sassy but playful tone. They stepped into the elevator, which whisked them to the top floor. When they stepped out, Peter knew exactly where to go.

"How long have you been planning this?" Meredith said.

Peter just looked at her and, with his hand, pretended to zip his mouth shut and throw away the key. This generated another eye roll from Meredith, but she was also exhilarated at the prospect of staying in a hotel for the first time with the man she was falling in love with.

The room was beyond anything she could have expected. The decor was French provincial, and the view was utter perfection. Even though it was a cloudy day, they could see the outline of magnificent Mount Hood, as well as the Willamette River snaking through downtown Portland.

Meredith turned just as the bellman closed the door. She did not hear a thing he said about the amenities of the hotel. She wanted to remember exactly how she felt, since she suspected this was going to be a very important day for her. She was ready to give herself to Peter, and she wanted to study every detail so she would never forget. The week prior they had talked openly about the issue of birth control, and Meredith had confided in him that she was ready, but wanted their first time to be memorable.

Peter put her small bag in the corner and smiled. They clung to each other as the door closed. The energy in the room became increasingly palpable, so much so that they frantically undressed without diverting their eyes from one another. Peter pulled the covers back, and they collapsed on the crisp sheets with anticipation. Neither could wait any longer. His hands touched her with what felt like electricity, and she moaned with delight as he introduced her to the passion that she had never known before. He slid his hands under her, and she was surprisingly unafraid. She knew Peter would be kind, making her first experience special. She loved him so much, and felt grateful that she had saved herself.

They never left the suite, and when it was time for dinner they feasted on omelets and champagne, with chocolate-dipped strawberries for dessert. The perfect meal capped off by a night of passion. Both knew that their relationship was forever sealed, and they would always be together.

Chapter 4

The following morning they awoke to a perfectly sunny February day—an anomaly in Portland, where the blustery rainy weather typically dragged on well into June. As the room-service attendant arrived with coffee and scones, Meredith gazed out the window, admiring the perfect view of the city. She had lived in Portland her entire life, and never before had it seemed so spectacular. It occurred to her that her life would never be the same again. *She* would never be the same again.

The clock read 7:35, and Peter and Meredith sadly acknowledged that their magical night was about to come to an end. But it really was just the beginning of a life together that would be filled with love and companionship.

They departed the Benson and walked hand in hand to Meredith's loft so she could change and be at work by nine. Peter grabbed a second cup of coffee from the bakery in Meredith's building and kept her company as she dressed for her day.

In the coming weeks, they spent quiet evenings at Meredith's quaint loft. They could barely finish dinner before tearing off their clothes, finding new ways to please each other. It seemed that they would never tire of each other's company, and they agreed that they should consider moving in together at some point in the not-too-distant future. Both had small apartments, so the first matter of business was to find a suitable place that could accommodate both of their furnishings. Luckily, they had similar tastes, so it would not be difficult to furnish. They agreed that a two-bedroom loft with a large common area was a necessity, and the sooner the better.

Less than three weeks later, a larger loft became available on the second floor of Meredith's building, and they snatched it up. Chandler, who was pleased to say that he had introduced the couple, was more than happy to help them move in exchange for a home-cooked meal and a six-pack of Caldera IPA. The three of them had a lovely evening after a long day of moving, but Meredith had a strange feeling when, as she was clearing the table, Peter and Chandler began quietly discussing something in the other room. She hadn't seen Peter upset, and it seemed to her that he was becoming increasingly frustrated with Chandler. It was not long after that Chandler left rather suddenly.

"What's up with him?" Meredith asked.

"Oh, nothing." But she could tell Peter was not happy with their friend. He shrugged it off, and they managed to do an about-face, happily christening their new loft. It had only been five months since they first met, but to Meredith everything seemed perfect. She was living with the man she knew she would one day marry.

The exhausting weekend flew by, but by Sunday night the loft was totally organized, and they ordered Chinese and watched a movie. They had both decided to take Monday off, anticipating that they would need a day to rest after combining two households. At nearly ten o'clock the phone rang. It seemed strange that someone would call so late, and Meredith worried that something might have happened to her parents. She felt bad that she had not spent much time with them lately. But they understood, and they loved Peter. All they wanted for their daughter was for her to be happy.

"Hello?" Peter said. Meredith noticed that he instantly got the same look on his face as the night before when he and Chandler were talking. He walked into the den and closed the door. About forty-five minutes later, he emerged, though he said very little. Meredith did not know what to say, and was hurt when he rebuffed her attempts to talk to him.

The next day she got up earlier than usual and made a pot of coffee without first waking Peter. He sheepishly came into the kitchen, kissing her neck as she poured a bowl of cereal.

"I know I was being standoffish last night, Mer, and I'm sorry."

"Peter, we have to be honest with each other. Please don't cut me out."

"I know, I know," he said.

"So, what's the deal with Chandler?"

Peter took a deep breath, as if to prepare for what was about to come. He finally said, "He's in deep, Mer, and I am really concerned."

"What do you mean?"

"You can't tell anyone, but you know that case his boss is prosecuting involving the group of al-Qaeda operatives that tried to illegally cross over from Canada into the U.S. through the state of Washington?"

"Uh, yeah."

"Well, about a month ago he was approached out of the blue by some guy, and offered a shitload of money to shred the document that is going to be the smoking gun in the case."

"What? Peter, he could go to prison!"

"I know, Mer. And now he has confided in me, which makes me an accessory to this whole fucking thing. I honestly don't know what to do. If I go to the authorities, my friend goes to jail, and I become a target for the friggin' Taliban. And if I do nothing and the authorities find out I knew something, I could go to prison."

Peter paced frantically while spewing this insane barrage. It was as if he were reiterating the plot of a movie, yet there was nothing remotely fictitious about what he was saying. Neither Peter nor Meredith could wrap their heads around the fact that they had been placed right in the middle of a potential international incident.

"Peter, we need to call the FBI. This is nothing we should mess around with. The government will protect us if we just come forward and do the right thing. Shit, Peter! Why didn't you tell me last night?" Meredith was so angry, she stormed into the bathroom and slammed the door.

"I'm sorry, Mer." But she was already running a bath and he knew his apology, while sincere, was not appreciated. Peter allowed her time to calm down, taking the opportunity to think through their options.

She emerged an hour later, and it was visible that she had been crying. They hugged tightly, well aware that they would have to be smart about their next move.

"I've given this some thought, Mer. I owe it to Chandler to tell him that we are going to the authorities, but I agree that telling the FBI is the smart thing to do."

"I cannot tell you how happy that makes me, Peter." Meredith sighed, feeling a huge sense of relief.

"I sent him a text while you were in the bathtub, and told him that I had to see him tonight. I haven't heard back yet," Peter said with frustration. "Ugh, where are you, Chandler?"

"Maybe we should go to his apartment and wait for him?" Meredith suggested.

Electing to call in sick to their respective employers, they waited nervously all day, but never heard from Chandler. By evening they both had a very bad feeling about the whole thing.

"You wait here, Mer. I'll go," Peter said. And with that he quickly kissed her forehead and grabbed his coat.

Meredith became increasingly worried when Peter did not call or text, but she decided not to bother him. She fell asleep on the couch and awoke suddenly at four o'clock, terrified that she had not received any word.

"Screw it," she said. And she grabbed her phone and called Peter. He answered on the first ring, and she heard a lot of commotion in the background.

"Peter, I'm so worried! Are you okay?"

Peter was audibly shaken. "Oh my God, Mer, it's worse than we thought."

Meredith stood paralyzed in the middle of their beautiful loft. Just yesterday she and Peter had made love on the floor here, in front of a roaring fireplace. How quickly things change, she thought.

"I will be home in a bit. I'll tell you everything when I get there." With that, the line went dead.

Within the hour, Peter walked through the door looking pale and terrified. Meredith sprinted to him, clinging like a frightened child.

"This is such a bad situation, Meredith. I got there right after these goons, who came out of nowhere, literally broke down Chandler's front door. If I had gotten there any sooner, I would probably be dead right now." As he said the words, tears welled up in his eyes. "Mer, Chandler's dead. They shot him in the head, and then fucking decimated his entire apartment!"

"Oh my gosh, Peter! What did you do?"

"I hid outside the window, but I saw the whole damn thing. It was like watching a scene from a movie or something. Mer, they went through all of his drawers, his computer, and just left. The place was a wreck, and Chandler just lay there bleeding with his eyes wide open. I seriously don't think I will ever be able to get that image out of my head." With his head in his hands, Peter dissolved into tears.

"Did they see you, Peter?"

"I don't think so, but I'm not sure how much they fucking know. I know this for sure, they seemed really pissed when they left. They were definitely looking for something, and whatever it was, they didn't find it."

"Peter, we have to call the police or the FBI or something."

"I agree. We'll go first thing in the morning."

And with that they went to bed, wishing they could rewind their life twenty-four hours. They managed to eventually fall asleep, but they awoke exhausted after only sleeping on and off for a few hours. They showered and went immediately to the FBI to file a report.

"How can I help you," said the woman at the information desk. She didn't bother to look up when she spoke.

"We need to speak with someone about a possible incident of, um, terrorism."

That seemed to get her attention. She looked back and forth from Peter to Meredith while grabbing her phone. She spoke quietly, and within two minutes an FBI agent surfaced to escort them to a conference room.

"I'm Agent Murino. Can I get either of you some coffee?"

"That would be great," Meredith said. She was in dire need of caffeine and could feel a pounding headache coming on.

Agent Murino poured each a cup of coffee and offered them a place at a ridiculously long conference table. Meredith could not help but wonder how many important people had sat at this table discussing national affairs.

"I understand you have some information about a terror threat. Can you be more specific?"

Peter cleared his throat and started from the beginning. He told Agent Murino every last detail. The last thing he wanted was the FBI to suspect that they had anything to do with Chandler and his connection to al-Qaeda.

"We know most of what you just told me, Mr. Delaney. Your friend was more involved than you could ever imagine. Judging from your story, you are very lucky that you arrived when you did last night, or you would probably be dead, too."

Meredith's eyes filled with tears at the thought. She had no idea how they'd even gotten to this place, but she was glad they had made the decision to contact the authorities.

"I am not at liberty to go into any specifics of the case. However, we can provide you with protection until the conclusion of the trial. After the trial is over, you're on your own," Agent Murino said, looking up briefly from his notes.

Peter looked terrified. "Wait. Are we in danger?"

"While we can't say for certain, I wouldn't be too worried. Based on your statement, you only became aware of Mr. Harris's involvement a short time ago. We have no reason to believe that the people involved knew you had any knowledge of the plot to destroy evidence."

Meredith and Peter left the FBI building and walked home without saying anything. Both were spent, and simply wanted the whole thing to go away. But later that day after they had managed to sleep, they resurfaced grateful that the events of the night had not turned out differently.

"I am so glad you were not hurt last night, Peter. I can't tell you how worried I was not knowing what was happening."

"I know, Mer. It's over now, and we can move on. Well, once the funeral is over. I should really call Chandler's parents and pass along my condolences."

"Maybe you should wait and see if there's anything in the newspaper before you do anything."

"Not a bad idea. I'll wait and see what the obituary says before I call."

The local paper ran a sizable article, as well as a photograph. Chandler had become the victim of a gruesome murder while working on a case that had gripped much of America. There was some commentary, but no mention was made of the fact that the crime scene had been wiped clean of any evidence. The article also held back the fact that Chandler had engaged in an apparent bribe in exchange for destroying documents. The government did not want the issue of evidence tampering to create a public relations nightmare for its high-profile case.

During the funeral, Chandler was hailed as a hero for his work with the prosecutor's office. Everyone was there, and it was clear that nobody had a clue that he had been involved in any way with the defendants. Peter immediately spotted Agent Murino, who sat in the back, carefully surveying the church.

"Look who's here," Peter whispered to Meredith.

"Why is he here? Do you think Chandler's murderer would have the nerve to show up at the funeral?"

"I don't know. I certainly hope not, anyway."

Following the service, they paid their respects to Mr. and Mrs. Harris and left the church before the reception commenced. There was something creepy about the energy in the room. Meredith figured it was because they knew more than anyone else, and it frankly made her sick to listen to the ongoing eulogies touting the heroism of a man who had put so many innocent people in danger.

They returned home, where they spent a quiet evening, agreeing to put the whole thing behind them. All they wanted to do was move forward with their life together.

Chapter 5

The weeks and months following the death of Chandler Harris were uneventful, and this made Peter and Meredith abundantly grateful. They knew they were being followed by the FBI, but they did not allow this to disrupt their personal and professional lives. They simply chose to think of it as a minor inconvenience.

As the trial drew near they both had feelings of trepidation, but they agreed they were not going to exert much energy on the salacious stories that consumed the local news. They knew too much already and had faith that the government would prevail in the end.

Just as they had hoped, the three-month trial moved along quickly, and all six defendants were easily convicted. Peter and Meredith were thrilled, and they decided to celebrate the fact that their nightmare was finally over.

They walked hand in hand to the waterfront and dined outside under the stars. It was a perfect summer evening. Peter always said you could not beat Portland on a beautiful summer day. Unfortunately, the other nine months of the year Oregonians paid the price with the seemingly endless rain. Peter and Meredith splurged and drank martinis with their appetizers, followed by a bottle of pinot noir and a delicious salmon dinner. Feeling more than tipsy, they laughed all the way home, knowing that they would not be going to sleep anytime soon. The last several months had been stressful, and neither Peter nor Meredith had much energy after putting in long days at work while making every effort to ignore the details of the trial, which were splashed across every international publication and cable news network. But now that the case was over, they wanted to make up for lost time. Meredith sat on Peter's lap and began unbuttoning his shirt, kissing his neck and behind his ear. She could tell he was incredibly aroused.

"Meredith, what did I ever do to deserve you?"

As he said that, she began kissing his chest. She could tell that the lower she went, the more he wanted her. She unzipped his jeans, feeling unusually adventurous, clearly surprising Peter with her sexual prowess.

"Meredith, I love you so much." And with that he reciprocated, giving her a mind-blowing finish that topped off the evening with perfection.

They made love again in the shower, then fell happily asleep. They woke the next morning feeling that they were the luckiest two people on earth. They dressed and went to the Heathman for brunch. After their long night they were famished, both ordering blueberry pancakes, bacon, and a huge pot of coffee. On the way home they did some shopping, and then ducked into a matinee to see the newest Diane Keaton film. With an exaggerated eye roll, Meredith could tell Peter was not especially excited to spend his afternoon at a chick flick, but he relented in the end, acknowledging that he knew Meredith had been dying to see it. When the movie was over and the lights went up, he agreed the movie was very funny, and they walked home reviewing their favorite scenes.

The next week was a busy one for both. Peter had a huge case going to trial, and Meredith was meeting with a new author who seemed especially impressive. When she arrived home on Wednesday evening, she was surprised to see their front door ajar. She did not think much about it, figuring Peter must not have closed it tightly when he got home.

"Hello?" she said. "I'm home. Peter?"

At that moment he walked through the door, causing Meredith to jump and let out a scream.

"A little jumpy?"

"Peter, are you just getting home?"

"Yeah, why?"

"Because I just got home and the door was open."

"You mean unlocked or actually open?"

"No, Peter, it was open!"

They stared at each other. Meredith instinctively began wringing her hands. "Peter, this is not good. Should we call the FBI?"

"And tell them what?" Putting his fingers to his ear to simulate a telephone receiver, he said, "Hi, FBI? So, here's the thing, our door was ajar and we would like you to send someone over right away to check it out."

Meredith stood with her hands on her hips, not at all amused.

"Tell you what, Mer, let's start by making sure nothing is missing."

Meredith gazed around the room. It all looked exactly as it had been twelve hours earlier when they left for work. They spent an hour scouring the loft, pulling out drawers and double-checking files. They established, in the end, that everything was in place and accounted for.

"Hey, I have an idea," Meredith said in a high-pitched squeal. "Let's go down to the bakery. Maybe they saw something!" She was certain she had stumbled upon a moment of genius.

"Mer, don't you think they have better things to do than monitor every person who walks in and out of the building?"

"Well, I'm going." And with that Meredith ran out of the loft and down the stairs.

"Ugh," Peter said as he raked his hands through his hair. He reluctantly descended the stairs, to at least appear that he supported Meredith's brilliant plan. After just a few steps, he ran into the on-site manager, who was on his way up the narrow stairway.

"Hi, Mark," Peter said. "Let me ask you something. Did you, by any chance, see anyone enter our apartment today?"

"The only person I saw was your college friend," Mark said.

Peter stood momentarily paralyzed. "What are you talking about, Mark?"

Mark snapped his fingers in the air, as if to help him think quicker. "Oh, yeah. Simon."

"Simon? I don't know anybody by the name of Simon. What did this guy look like?" Peter said.

"Tall, well-dressed, a little too much cologne for my taste; kind of international-looking. He seemed nice, though. He had a key so I didn't give it much thought. Are you sure you don't know this guy? On second thought, maybe he said he was friends with Meredith." And with that, Mark excused himself to take care of a backed-up sink on the next floor. Peter stood there, staring at nothing, unable to believe what Mark had said.

"Well, they didn't see anything," Meredith said, taking two steps at a time. "Maybe we're making too big a deal of this, and we just didn't close it tightly when we left this morning."

Peter mentioned nothing to Meredith about his conversation, but became unusually distracted during the course of the evening.

"What's up with you tonight?" Meredith finally said.

"I'm sorry, Mer. I am dealing with a stressful client, who is driving me nuts."

With no reason to think otherwise, she cut him some slack and cleaned up the kitchen, allowing Peter to retreat to the den to be alone.

Chapter 6

The night seemed endless to Peter. As the sun came up he slipped out of bed to make a pot of coffee, methodically jotting down a few notes about the events of the prior day. He was feeling increasingly nervous and did not want to forget anything during his meeting with the FBI.

"What are you doing up so early, Peter? You thrashed about all night long!"

Clearly startled, Peter jumped while pulling the notebook under the table.

"Uh, nothing."

"Nothing? Come on, Peter. You don't have to show me if you don't want to, but I don't believe for a minute it's nothing."

"Really, Mer. It's just a, uh, that work thing I was telling you about, and you startled me when you came in."

She smiled and straddled him, tossing the notebook across the room. "We don't have to be at work for a few hours. Want to go back to bed?"

"Tempting as it may be, Mer, I have a big meeting, which is why I was up so early."

"Okay, but you're missing out," she said, as she allowed her bathrobe to casually open, showing her terrific figure.

Peter scooped up the notebook, which had slid under the fridge, and stuffed it in his briefcase as Meredith poured herself a cup of coffee. He quickly showered and dressed for the day. She had the feeling that something was up, but she shook it off and flipped on *Good Morning America* as the door slammed shut a few minutes later.

The morning dragged on, and even a venti coffee wasn't enough to keep Meredith focused on her manuscript. Luckily, her afternoon client called to reschedule, which was a huge relief considering she was running on fumes after enduring a painful night's sleep with Peter constantly tossing and turning. Just as her favorite sushi bar arrived with her mid-week guilty pleasure, she was surprised to see Peter close behind.

"Hey, sweetie. What are you doing here? I thought you had some big meeting today," Meredith said, already noshing on her first piece of sashimi.

"I did, Mer. But I wasn't totally honest with you earlier. I met with Agent Murino this morning."

"What do you mean, Peter?"

"Any chance you can cut out early today? You are not going to like what I have to say."

Abandoning the rest of her lunch, Meredith took the rest of the day off, and they went home to talk privately. Peter filled her in on the conversation he had with Mark the day before. While she was angry he didn't initially confide in her, she could at least appreciate the fact that his intentions were pure.

"So that's what you were doing up at the crack of dawn this morning," she said, still trying to digest everything Peter was telling her.

"I just wanted to make sure I told the FBI everything. Honestly, as I was going through my notes with Agent Murino, I couldn't believe we were back where we first started when this whole thing went down with Chandler.

"So, what did Agent Murino say?"

"He said that they recently received some intelligence that two operatives connected to the case still remained in the area. Luckily, the FBI has agreed to put two agents in front of our building until they can determine who this Simon guy is, and why he paid us a visit. He also asked if there was anything I could think of in the loft that could be of interest."

"Like what?"

"I have no fucking idea. I mean, Chandler was here once."

"This is insane, Peter. Should we move again?"

"Mer, the FBI is handling it. Let's just trust that they will take care of it."

"I don't like this, Peter." Tears streamed from Meredith's eyes as she dropped her head into her hands.

Peter took Meredith in his arms and held her tight. They went to bed that night feeling some sense of relief thanks to the two FBI agents outside their front door, but they had no idea how the whole thing would play out in the end.

A week later, Peter received a call from Agent Murino, advising him that they had caught the man who'd entered the apartment. He was a member of an underground al-Qaeda cell and had been taken into custody. However, they had not been able to glean any specific information about the connection to Peter or Meredith. Agent Murino did say that he would continue to have them followed by the FBI until they resolved the case.

Though they felt like they might never find a way out, Peter and Meredith decided to do what they had done before the trial. They were going to live their lives and let the FBI handle the details of the investigation.

Chapter 7

Before they knew it, they were celebrating the one-year anniversary of the day they met. They toasted with martinis at the VQ, giving a special toast to their friend who had sadly lost his life in exchange for a senseless bribe. Regardless of his involvement, he had brought the happy couple together, and for that they would always be grateful.

When the waitress brought a second round, Meredith looked down, and then back up at Peter with a smile. Dangling from the swizzle stick perched in her martini was a beautiful platinum diamond ring.

"Meredith Singler, will you marry me?"

Meredith said, "Peter Delaney, I absolutely will marry you."

Peter happily slid the ring onto the finger of the woman he'd fallen in love with exactly one year before.

They walked home hand in hand, totally oblivious to the familiar Oregon rain, which drenched them from head to toe. They had never been so happy, even though behind them walked two FBI agents tasked with ensuring that they arrived home safely.

"You wanna try and ditch them, Mer? Let's see just how fast Larry and Mo can run." Peter always called them that, and Meredith could not help laughing every time.

"Um, no," Meredith said with sarcasm dripping from her lips. "That's all we need, Peter. To lose our goon patrol, and arrive home to find the long-lost cousin of Osama bin Laden waiting for us in our loft!"

Peter laughed, and kissed the new hardware on her left hand.

Meredith's parents insisted on giving the couple an engagement party at their sprawling home, which overlooked the lights of downtown Portland. The gathering included 150 of their longtime friends, as well as all of Meredith's and Peter's friends and colleagues. Peter's entire family flew in from the East Coast to celebrate the upcoming nuptials. It was an exciting time, and everyone was ecstatic for the happy couple. Only Peter and Meredith knew about the dark cloud that continued to loom over them, and they had decided there was no need to unnecessarily alarm their friends and family.

They arrived home feeling blissful. Peter turned off the lights and slid into bed, pulling Meredith close. He made his intentions clear as he pulled off her silky camisole and discarded it on the floor. Meredith responded by wrapping her long legs around him. She was so turned on by him that she instinctively took control. Peter found it intoxicating when Meredith took the initiative, anticipating exactly what would drive him crazy. They both fell asleep completely exhausted yet perfectly satisfied.

Chapter 8

The winter flew by, and everything seemed to be status quo. Larry and Mo were no longer needed, and Peter and Meredith were happy to plan their wedding, which exceeded three hundred guests. Neither really wanted a huge wedding, but they felt pressure because they were both only children and both sets of parents desperately wanted this to be a grand occasion.

The big day finally came and Portland gladly cooperated; it was a breezy, seventy-degree June afternoon without a hint of rain. The wedding took place at Meredith's childhood church. The historic First Presbyterian Church was located on the corner of 12th and Alder, which made it easy for the guests to transition to the reception at the Benson, a few blocks away. The famed hotel held great memories for Peter and Meredith, and they would later celebrate their wedding night in the same suite in which they had initially sealed their commitment to each other.

At some point during the spectacular celebration, while the guests drank champagne and danced well into the morning hours, Peter and Meredith sneaked upstairs to start their honeymoon. It had taken what seemed like a lifetime for Meredith to find the perfect dress, yet neither could wait for her to shed the layers of tulle and French lace as the doors to the familiar suite closed behind them. Underneath, she was wearing a satin bustier and matching bikini panties. It was a bit of a splurge, but she figured it would set the tone for their romantic honeymoon, and she was right. Peter and Meredith happily became man and wife over and over that night, as the party continued just a few floors below.

The next day, the hotel was more than pleased to accommodate the happy couple with a late checkout and arrange for a town car to take them to the airport. They had purposely booked a flight in the afternoon, anticipating that they would be incredibly tired.

"Is that what I think it is?"

While Meredith was in the shower, Peter had ducked out to surprise his bride with her most favorite shameful indulgence before heading to the airport. He stood in the doorway to the grand bathroom, holding a pink box; on the lid was the familiar insignia of Voodoo Doughnuts, a Portland favorite that offered a crazy selection of the most unique sugary delicacies.

"Please tell me you got my favorite," she said, clapping her hands.

"One maple bar with bacon at your service, Mrs. Delaney."

"I love the way that sounds," she giggled, and she took a huge bite, acting like she was going to faint. "I can't wait to get to San Francisco," she chirped.

"You know, Mer, we could have gone anywhere in the world. I think it's funny you want to go to the Bay Area."

"What? It's only the most romantic place ever!"

Peter chuckled. "It doesn't matter to me. If I have my way, we won't see the light of day anyway."

As they checked in at Southwest Airlines, Meredith could not help but notice a woman who seemed to be staring at her.

"Peter, don't be obvious, but is that lady over by the pillar staring at us?"

"What lady, Mer?"

But when Meredith turned to look again, the woman was no longer there.

"I think you're tired and in need of a vacation, Mrs. Delaney." And with that, he kissed her in the middle of the Portland airport, not caring what anyone else thought.

They boarded the plane, excited at the prospect of ten days with nothing to do. They planned to spend the first few days in the city, then rent a car and spend the last week in Sonoma. The weather was going to be spectacular, and they could not wait to lounge by the pool and drink wine at the local vineyards.

On their way from the airport to the famous Mark Hopkins Hotel, Meredith told Peter a story about her grandmother as a young woman just starting out after graduating from college. It was 1923, and Meredith's grandmother, who was always known for being spunky and chic, had gotten a job as a teacher at a fancy private school in San Francisco. Every weekend, she and her friends gathered at the Top of the Mark for cocktails.

"You know, Peter, that was during Prohibition. She was so ahead of her time," she said, smiling at the thought. "I love that my grandmother was a rebel," Meredith said, raising an eyebrow.

"Hmm, I guess the apple didn't fall far from the tree," Peter said, sliding his hand up her skirt.

"Hey, we're here," Meredith announced, as their town car came to a stop.

The hotel was magnificent. The lobby had been refurbished the prior year, and it was beautifully appointed with clusters of sofas and small tables that encouraged guests to gather. The huge chandeliers were like works of art, and they shimmered as the sun from the skylights bounced off the individual crystals. Massive vases of fresh flowers peppered the grand lobby, giving the hotel a boutique feel. Meredith was pleased, and could not wait to see their room.

The bellman flipped on the light and politely held the door for them to enter, and their jaws simultaneously dropped. The suite was a smaller version of the lobby, and Meredith jumped up and down, clapping her hands like a child. Though trying to remain reserved, the hotel employee clearly got a kick out of her exuberance, winking at Peter as he handed him the key cards.

Once they were alone, Peter flung open the curtains, revealing an unbelievable view of San Francisco. The historic hotel had the appearance of being sandwiched between the Golden Gate Bridge and Coit Tower. It was so much more than they'd hoped for. Meredith quietly acknowledged how grateful she was for her happiness.

"Peter, I love you so much," she whispered. And with that, they peeled off their clothes and passionately made love.

"I don't know who ever said it was all downhill after the wedding," Peter teased. They could not get enough of each other, eventually falling asleep under the feather duvet.

The morning brought misty skies, but the fog eventually burned off and the day ended up sunny and cool. Meredith had been to San Francisco with her parents several times before, and she knew the city like the back of her hand. They had a beautiful breakfast at her favorite restaurant near the water and then walked the full length of Crissy Field, admiring Alcatraz in the distance.

"Hey, let's get some lunch at the Warming Hut," Meredith suggested. The long swath of grass ended at a small sandy beach, where a small cottage served a beautiful menu of gourmet lunch items, including the best soup in the city.

"How do you know about this place, Mer? It looks like a boathouse or something."

"Oh, I get around," Meredith said in a husky whisper.

He slapped her fanny and grabbed her hand as they walked into the charming cafe. It actually looked very much like a boathouse inside, eclectic, with a dash of casual sophistication. In addition to the beautiful menu, they sold a lovely collection of books, high-end pottery, and European kitchen utensils. Meredith was in heaven as she perused the unique wares and thumbed through the cookbooks that lined the shelves.

They took their lunch outside and found a place on the low rock wall near the crashing waves from the bay. The weather was perfect, and they chatted happily about what they should do that evening. Earlier that morning, the concierge had suggested a few options available in and around the city, and Peter had made arrangements for two orchestra seats to see the San Francisco Opera perform *La Bohème*. Meredith was thrilled when he told her, and even more excited when he whisked her to Neiman Marcus to splurge on a new outfit for their night out.

With two hours to spare before their dinner reservations at RN74, the award-winning Michael Mina restaurant Meredith's parents had insisted they try, Peter and Meredith showered together.

"Now this is what I call killing two birds with one stone," Peter said as he gently pushed Meredith against the tile wall. He was always ready to go, and she was equally turned on by her sexy husband. They lingered in the steamy shower, finding the multi-spray feature especially erotic. "Remind me to have one of these showers installed when we get home," Peter whispered.

"I'm pretty sure this shower is bigger than our whole kitchen, Peter."

"Kitchens are overrated anyway. Let's just convert it into a shower, and we'll order in from now on."

And with that they made love again, realizing that they had better hurry or they would miss dinner.

Chapter 9

*S*aying goodbye to San Francisco was difficult, but they both looked forward to spending the next week in the heart of wine country. They anticipated warm days and cool nights, which sounded perfect to both of them. They had reserved a bungalow at the chic but comfortable El Dorado Hotel, which was located right on the town square in charming Sonoma.

Navigating their way over the Golden Gate Bridge in their rented red convertible, they could feel the sun getting warmer and warmer with every passing mile. They drank in the marine air of Marin County and, as they passed Sausalito, decided to look for a quick place for lunch. Reviews on Yelp pointed them to a small cafe in Larkspur, right off 101. They easily found a parking place on Magnolia Street, and Meredith told Peter she thought she could fall in love with this adorable town.

"Even the street names are beautiful," she exclaimed.

After lunching on Brie-and-Black-Forest-ham sandwiches, they both felt much happier, and decided that they were in no hurry to leave the quaint town of Larkspur. They ducked in and out of the high-end shops, and Meredith was sure she had found nirvana in the Coquelicot boutique. She spoke with the owner in French and learned that the name of the store was a French vernacular for the fiery orange and red poppies that peppered the Bay Area. Peter found her second language to be incredibly sexy. As they left, Meredith turned and casually said, *"A tout à l'heure, Madame."*

"That was hot, Mer. I love listening to you speak French. That was French, right?"

Meredith laughed. *"Oui."* She held her hand up in the air, as if to jokingly simulate smoking a cigarette.

They eventually left for Sonoma, but promised they would return to Larkspur one day. There was something special about it, and both Peter and Meredith felt a connection to the people and the Zen energy of Marin County.

The rest of the week flew by, and they enjoyed every minute of it, lying poolside and touring numerous wineries. Just before they left, Peter slipped a flat square box into Meredith's hand.

"What's this, Peter?"

"Open it," he said with a sly smile.

"Peter! When did you get this?" A few days before, while at a local art studio, she had admired the painting of red poppies, but she'd opted to pass because she thought it was too expensive.

"Oh, I managed to sneak out one morning while you were at the spa. I could tell how much you loved it, and I wanted you to have something special to remind you of our honeymoon."

"I will never forget this trip. And now I have these beautiful poppies to remind me every day. Thank you, Peter. I couldn't love it more."

They spent one last night blissfully making love in their beautiful suite, wishing they could stay on their honeymoon forever. They ended their trip tan and rested. It was the perfect vacation, and they agreed they should return to the Bay Area to celebrate their first anniversary.

Chapter 10

The flight back to Portland was quick and uneventful. A prearranged town car picked them up, and they arrived home in a matter of minutes. As they approached their apartment, Meredith saw a light on inside their loft. They had been in such a rush before the wedding, she figured they had inadvertently left a light on. But she could not help but acknowledge that ever-present voice in the back of her head, questioning whether she and Peter would ever be safe after the months of chaos they had endured.

Peter scooped Meredith up as they got to the door, and carried her over the threshold. Meredith, laughing hysterically, managed to wiggle out of his arms as they entered the familiar apartment. It seemed like forever since they had been home, and they were shocked by the stacks of gifts that lined the walls. Her parents had been kind enough to deliver the presents and organize the arsenal of packages in a way that would make the exciting task easy to complete.

"I have to be honest, Peter. I had a moment of panic when I looked up from the street and saw a light on in the loft. I'm sure my dad forgot to turn the hall light off when they stopped by," Meredith said.

"Mer, we have to move on. We have a lot of work to do," he said in a very serious tone.

"Work?"

He pulled her J.Crew sweater over her head, kissing her neck. They never even made it to the bedroom, and Meredith forgot all about who might have left the light on.

"I like this kind of work," she said as they lingered in bed all morning.

They took the rest of the week off, knowing they would have gifts to open and thank-you notes to compose. It was so much more than either Peter or Meredith could have expected, and they were blown away by the generosity of their friends and family.

In a matter of three days, Meredith and Peter had opened the gifts, discarded the boxes and mounds of tissue paper, and made a small dent in their thank-you notes.

"I'll tell you what I am going to give as a wedding gift from now on," Peter said.

"What's that?"

"A cleanup crew to come in after the gifts are opened," he joked.

"No kidding," she said, laughing.

They met a group of Meredith's friends at Huber's Cafe for Spanish coffees that evening, and chatted for almost three hours about their magical honeymoon. Meredith's friends loved Peter, and thought it was so sweet that he had given her an original painting as a wedding gift. While Meredith knew they were genuinely happy for her, they could not help but express a little envy. They all complained about how difficult it was to be single in Portland, and made it abundantly clear that they would be open to blind dates if Peter had any single friends.

That night Meredith confided in Peter how grateful she was to have found him; she could not imagine loving him more than she loved him at that moment. Peter smiled, clearly touched as Meredith's tears spilled onto her pillow.

They had one last weekend before returning to work. Even though they adored their time together, both Peter and Meredith were anxious to get on with their individual lives. They loved their respective careers, and prided themselves on hard work and the accomplishments they achieved in their jobs.

First thing Saturday morning, they met Meredith's parents for brunch at the Benson. So many special memories made it one of their favorite spots in Portland. Dr. and Mrs. Singler toasted the newlyweds with mimosas, acknowledging how thrilled they were for the happy couple. Meredith appreciated that they had shown restraint when it came to the looming question of grandchildren. While they rarely pried, she could tell they desperately wanted an approximate baby timeline. They had saved all of Meredith's favorite childhood treasures and made it clear they could not wait to introduce the familiar toys and books to their first grandchild.

Happily arriving home, Peter grabbed the sports section and planted himself on the sofa to watch the University of Oregon play in a preseason exhibition game.

"No Oregon Duck fans in this house. We root for Stanford!" Meredith fake-screamed.

Peter laughed, electing not to tell her that there was no better football team than the Oregon Ducks, and no way Stanford would even make it to a bowl game that season. As Meredith walked past the fireplace, she noticed that her martini painting had been removed; it was perched on the mantel against the wall.

"Peter, did you take my painting off the wall?"

"Um, huh," he said, continuing to read the prior day's stats.

"Peter, someone took my painting off the wall."

"That's weird," Peter said without looking up.

"It's more than weird, Peter. Peter! Are you listening to me?"

Peter finally folded the paper. "Yes, Mer, I am at full attention." But as quickly as he'd looked up, he was distracted by something under the armoire. Half listening to Meredith, he walked across the room and grabbed what looked like a credit card from under Meredith's favorite antique.

"What's that?"

"Well, it looks like a credit card, but I think it's some type of identification card." He flipped the card over. Meredith peeked over his shoulder and gasped at the sight of the tiny photo in the bottom corner of the card. Next to the photo was a name that neither could pronounce, but it appeared to be Arabic.

"Oh my god, Peter, that was the woman at the airport!"

Peter looked completely confused.

"Remember the day we left for San Francisco? Remember when I asked you if that woman by the pillar was staring at us? That's her, Peter!"

"Meredith, how can you possibly remember a woman you saw for a split second? Don't you think you're being a little hasty?"

"No, Peter, I don't," Meredith said curtly. "I'm going to the FBI right now."

"Okay, tell you what. I'm pretty sure they're closed on Saturday," Peter said with the slightest hint of humorous sarcasm in his voice. "I will make an appointment with Agent Murino. After all, Mer, we can't just keep showing up at the FBI unannounced and not expect them to think we're nuts."

During their last interaction, Agent Murino had given Peter his cell number in case he needed to contact him after hours. Peter pulled up the number and sent the agent a text.

"Let's try to remain calm, Mer. There's no reason to freak out."

But as he said the words, Meredith just shook her head and said, "Peter, why the fuck would this woman's identification card be in our loft, and why has my painting been pulled off the wall?"

Not twenty minutes later, Agent Murino called, and they scheduled a meeting for the following Monday. He mentioned to Peter that he had been planning to contact them because the FBI had recovered some additional information from Chandler's apartment and wanted to know if Peter or Meredith could shed some light on the situation.

Chapter 11

*P*eter and Meredith arrived well before their nine o'clock appointment, both a little nervous. In an effort to be funny and lighthearted, Peter said to the receptionist, "We really need to stop meeting like this."

Without cracking a smile, she said, "You can wait in the lobby," and immediately went back to work.

"Wow, Peter, you certainly have a way with the ladies!" Meredith teased.

Peter rolled his eyes. "Oh, you're so funny!"

"Mr. and Mrs. Delaney?"

Peter and Meredith looked up to see Agent Murino. Passing on small talk and coffee, they settled into the familiar conference room.

"So, tell me what's going on."

Meredith told him about her experience at the airport, as well as arriving home to find the identification card, and the painting out of place. Agent Murino sat quietly, listening to every detail and taking copious notes as Peter and Meredith recounted the story. During a pause in the conversation, he cleared his throat and lightly tapped his pen on his notes.

"Now, I don't want to alarm you, but we recovered something troubling from Chandler Harris's apartment. A flash drive was found in a wall safe, and one of the documents it contained made reference to both of you."

"What do you mean? We had no idea Chandler was involved with anything illegal until the day before his death," Meredith said.

"The information we received does not point to your involvement per se. It turns out that Mr. Harris hid something in an unknown location that could be very, let's say, detrimental, to the parties of the case."

"Wait a minute. So, was Chandler the good guy or the bad guy?"

"We're not sure yet, Mr. Delaney. We'd like to have your permission to have our team of investigators inspect your loft to see if we can find anything."

Peter took a moment. Then, "And what if we say no, Agent Murino?"

"We can always get a search warrant, Mr. Delaney."

Meredith could not believe how quickly the conversation had deteriorated. In a matter of minutes they had gone from pleasantries to the threat of a search warrant. How had they arrived back here? She put both hands up to her temples, feeling the familiar signs indicating the dreaded onset of a migraine headache.

"Mr. and Mrs. Delaney, the FBI wants to protect you. We have no reason to believe either of you is involved."

"All right, but we both want to be present, and you're not turning our apartment upside down."

"Mr. Delaney, this is not the movies. All we want to do is look for clues that will allow us to close our case."

"Fine. We have the day off. Would today work for you?"

"How about noon? Oh, I am also going to need that identification card you found in your loft," Agent Murino said, in a way that gave them little choice in the matter.

Peter and Meredith relinquished the card and went home, trying to wrap their heads around the fact that a swarm of FBI agents would be descending upon their loft in a matter of hours.

"Maybe I should make coffee or something," Meredith said.

"Fuck no! We are not having an FBI tea party. I want them in and out as fast as possible, Mer."

"Well, I don't know the protocol of a federal investigation," she said, her voice at an unusually high pitch. She stood idle, looking around the room, hoping they would be careful during the search.

The hour approached, and as expected, there was a light knock at the door. Five men in dark suits walked in; they scoured the loft in less than an hour. "Mr. and Mrs. Delaney, your loft is clean from what we can tell. Until the case is closed, we will post an undercover agent outside your building."

After they left, Peter and Meredith stood motionless, looking at each other. They felt so violated. First by Chandler, then by the woman at the airport, and now by the FBI.

"I don't know, Mer. Something seems off."

"What do you mean, Peter?"

"I can't put my finger on it. I thought I heard two of the guys say something about checking behind the painting above the fireplace."

"Well, we did tell him that it was leaning against the wall when we came home from our trip. So it would make sense that they would inspect it. Right?"

"I guess," Peter said. "I just have a weird feeling."

In an effort to shake off the events of the day, they spent the rest of the afternoon exchanging duplicate wedding gifts, followed by a late lunch at Jake's. As they sat in a booth next to the window, they pretended that the FBI agent lurking outside the restaurant was just another guy on the street.

After lunch, they lost themselves in the Portland Art Museum. Both Peter and Meredith loved the newly refurbished gallery that housed some of their favorite artists, and for a few hours allowed themselves to drink in the lilies of Monet and the ballerinas that Degas had made so famous. Returning home was a sad reminder that they continued to be the targets of an international incident that simply would not seem to go away.

"I'm famished. I think I'll make an omelet," Meredith said, turning on a few lights. "Want one?"

"Sounds great." Peter turned on the TV and flipped through the channels, not really able to concentrate on anything. He looked at the martini painting across the room.

"What's the deal with this painting," he said under his breath. He crossed the room and took the painting off the wall, inspecting the front and back. Nothing seemed out of the ordinary. Why the hell was this painting such a point of interest for so many people?

Meredith came into the room with two plates. "What are you doing, Peter?"

"I just thought I'd take a closer look, since this painting keeps coming up in conversation."

"Hey, what happened to the frame?"

"What do you mean, Meredith?"

"It's cracked along the bottom. Damn it! That totally pisses me off. I bet they broke it when they were here today."

Peter turned the canvas upside down to see if there was a way he could fix the frame. Just as he put it down, Meredith noticed that something was lodged in a small hole that had been carved out at the bottom of the frame.

"Holy crap, Mer. I think you just found a motherfucking flash drive in the frame of your painting."

"Peter, we should call Agent Murino right away."

"Not until I see for myself what's on this thing." And with that Peter popped it into their computer.

"Oh my gosh, Peter. We could get in trouble," she said, anxiously pacing back and forth.

"Mer, they're not going to know. We'll call the FBI first thing in the morning. But for now, we are going to get some well-deserved answers to our unanswered questions."

Meredith couldn't believe what she saw on the screen. It was a journal. Chandler's journal, which chronicled the entire scenario, starting from the very beginning.

"Holy shit, Chandler was in deep, but look who was right along for the ride," Peter said. "I have had a weird feeling about Murino since the beginning. Ever notice that he always seemed to have conveniently uncovered a new lead every time we showed up with information? God, I feel like a fucking chump!"

"Oh my god, Peter. That's why Agent Murino wanted to inspect our loft. He must have known there was a flash drive containing Chandler's notes, but couldn't locate it in his apartment. The last thing he wants is to be implicated by a dead guy from the prosecutor's office. We are so lucky Chandler managed to hide it well. What should we do, Peter?"

"First thing in the morning, I'm going to call Brad Cunningham. He is an investigator who works for our firm. He's the best in the business, and very discreet."

Neither Peter nor Meredith slept that night. How could they still be in the middle of this nightmare? Meredith felt sick, physically sick, waking up every hour painfully reminded that they had fewer and fewer allies. In the morning she vomited after unsuccessfully trying to stomach a piece of toast.

"Are you okay, Mer?" Peter asked when she returned from the bathroom.

"Yeah, I feel better now. This whole thing is making me disgusted, Peter."

Peter left early, slipping past the FBI agent to run for the bus. He wanted to make a quick stop before meeting with the investigator. Now that he and Meredith were married, he felt it was his responsibility to protect her if the unimaginable happened. So he stopped off and met with the insurance agent who had sold them renters insurance after they moved in together. He opted to leave out the fact that he and Meredith were in the middle of an international incident. He simply said that they wanted to start a family sooner rather than later and thought that a life insurance policy would be a wise purchase.

A little after nine he walked into a packed Starbucks on the corner of Fourth and Broadway. He saw Brad Cunningham in the corner, and waved as he approached. Brad was well known as a thorough yet discreet private investigator, and was frequently utilized by Peter's firm on high-profile cases.

"Hey, Peter." They shook hands while Peter tried to force a smile. "Congratulations! I hear you got married."

"Thanks, Brad. Hey, I'm going to cut to the chase. I have a job for you."

"Sure, what's up?"

He confided in Brad, asking him to keep their troubles to himself. He had a bad feeling about the whole thing and especially wanted to protect Meredith.

"I saw the trial in the paper. Man, I had no idea you and your wife were involved," Brad said. "I'll see what I can find out, and get back to you as soon as I can."

Chapter 12

Two weeks passed, and both Peter and Meredith enjoyed the fact that their lives had at least some semblance of normalcy. That is, as long as they ignored the fact that they had in their possession an illegal flash drive, not to mention the two burly FBI agents, who remained parked outside their building, dutifully following them to and from work each day.

Peter's cell phone rang as he was preparing to leave the office one evening. At the last minute, he decided to answer it even though it was a blocked number.

"Hello?"

"Peter, it's Brad. Got a minute?"

"Sure. Where are you?"

"I'm in the lobby of your office building. Want to grab a beer, and hear the gory details?"

"I'll be right down."

Peter sent Meredith a text saying that he had to work late. He hated lying to her but did not want her to worry until he knew more.

"So, what did you find out?"

"Have a seat, Peter. What I have to tell you is really ugly."

They ordered IPAs and made sure nobody was close enough to hear their conversation. Peter's personal FBI escort was perched outside the bar, and the only person within earshot was a blond woman a few tables away, who seemed far more interested in her *People* magazine.

"All right, give it to me."

"Peter, you were right about Agent Murino. He's on the take, and the person at the other end of that payout is the woman your wife saw at the airport. She's the daughter of one of the defendants who went to prison, and she's not too happy that her family money was wasted on a deal gone bad. Both are trying to keep their involvement on the down-low. And that's why Chandler was killed," Brad said, taking a swig of his beer.

"Wait, so how is it that Murino is still standing?"

"Barely standing, Peter. He's doing what he can to save himself, but this is not a situation you want to be attached to. Besides Murino, you, Meredith, and yours truly are the only three who know."

"Oh my god, Brad. How do we know there aren't more at the FBI that are in on this?"

"He's the only one. I'm pretty sure of it."

"What should we do?"

"I'd say keep your head down. This woman is nobody you want to mess with. She's the daughter of the number-three most wanted al-Qaeda terrorist, and she is going to do whatever she can to stay in the shadows."

"How the fuck did this happen?" Peter said, looking up at the ceiling.

As they left the bar, neither noticed the blond wig that had been left behind in the garbage can next to the main entrance.

Peter told Meredith that night, and naturally she was upset. They decided they would take Brad's advice and lie low for a while, and the following weekend they got out of town. They arranged to spend three days in Coupeville, Washington, sans their FBI babysitter. Agent Murino initially disapproved, claiming it was not in their best interest to travel without protection, but he came around when Peter suggested that he would go over his head if necessary.

The charming town on Whidbey Island, located just off the coast, was exactly what they needed. Peter's colleague had offered his vacation home as a wedding gift, and this was the perfect opportunity to leave their problems behind for at least a few days. The weather was sunny and breezy, which allowed Peter and Meredith to spend lazy days on the deck and take romantic walks on the beach at sunset. Neither brought up their most recent scare. There was no reason to talk about it, since there was nothing they could do for the time being.

As they reluctantly boarded the ferry back to the mainland, Meredith experienced a familiar wave of nausea. She sat with her head in her hands for the better part of their trip home.

"Maybe you're pregnant, Mer."

She looked up, calculating the last time she'd had a period. With all the chaos of the wedding, and then the craziness of the FBI debacle, she honestly could not recall how long it had been.

Peter was thrilled at the prospect of a baby, but Meredith was not so sure. She loved her career and did not know how a baby would fit into their busy lives. Besides, they were still newlyweds, and she wanted to have plenty of time to make love on the kitchen floor if they wanted to.

They stopped in Seattle to eat, which Meredith hoped would make her feel better. While waiting for their sandwiches, they picked up a copy of the *Seattle Times*. Splashed across the front page, they were stunned to see the headline "FBI Loses Portland Agent."

The article indicated that Agent James Murino had been found dead in a random shooting. His body was found along the waterfront, and there were no suspects. It went on to say that the FBI was saddened by the events and would be conducting a full investigation.

"Peter, do you think it was that woman?"

"I wouldn't be surprised. After all, she's the offspring of one of the most wanted terrorists in Afghanistan. Killing is in her blood, Mer."

Meredith started to cry. "Is this ever going to end, Peter?"

"I'll call Brad in the morning and get the name of someone at the FBI who we can trust."

The next day Peter called Brad from his office and was surprised when Brad's wife answered. She sounded like she had been crying.

"Um, hi, this is Peter Delaney. Is Brad available?"

"Brad was shot last night, Peter. He apparently got in the middle of a federal investigation and never came home. This morning I received a call from the FBI, saying that he got mixed up with some high-profile case and was found dead under the Burnside Bridge. The only thing they know for sure is that whoever did it was a professional, because there was no evidence left behind." Barely able to utter the words, she dissolved into tears, unable to continue the conversation.

Peter could not wait to get off the phone. As far as he knew, he and Meredith were the last two who knew about the plot besides Number Three's kid.

"Fucking bitch," Peter said as he hung up. He spent the day trying to figure out a way out of this thing, and arrived home that evening to a candlelit dinner. Meredith was standing in the doorway, looking like the cat that swallowed the canary.

"What's this about?" Peter said, trying to sound like someone whose head was not next on the chopping block.

Meredith gave him a huge hug, then slipped a small box into his hand.

He put his briefcase down and sat down on the sofa. He untied the ribbon, opened the box, and pulled out a pair of tiny baby booties. Meredith just sat there, smiling with a slightly raised eyebrow, and nodded her head.

"Are you serious, Mer?"

And with that he put aside the events of the day and focused only on his beautiful wife.

Chapter 13

The following day they woke up to another gray, drizzly morning. Meredith was happily moving beyond the queasy phase and was famished. Peter was pleased to make her a huge breakfast. After all, she was carrying his baby, and he made it clear he wanted both to be safe and well fed.

As they sat down to eat, Peter knew he would have to tell Meredith about Brad sooner rather than later. There was a good chance it would be on the front page of the paper, and he did not want her to find out that way.

"Um, Mer? I have to tell you something. I don't want you to freak out, but Brad Cunningham's body was found under the Burnside Bridge while we were out of town. Now, it's not certain that there's a connection with our case, but . . ."

"It's that crazy al-Qaeda chick," Meredith interrupted. "I just know it, Peter. And we're next!" Meredith looked terrified, as her eyes filled with tears.

"Mer, we are not next. Brad felt certain that Murino was the only weak link at the FBI. Now listen to me. I have had a few conversations with our friends out front, and I am pretty sure we can trust him."

"Yeah, we thought we could trust Agent Murino, too!" Meredith said, flailing her arms in the air.

"Well, we don't really have much choice, with that whack job still out there."

Leaving much of their breakfast behind, they dressed and left the building, determined to seize control of a situation that they knew they had little command over. They nonchalantly asked their twenty-four-hour chaperones whom Agent Murino reported to at the agency.

"We all report directly to the chief. Her name is Marjorie La Croix. She's basically in charge of the Portland Bureau."

"Thanks," Meredith said. And with that, they went straight to the office of Chief La Croix. As they walked into the familiar lobby, Meredith said, "Hey, there's your girlfriend, Peter. Why don't you go sweet-talk her again?"

"Nice, Mer. A sense of humor, even in a time of international terror. I like that."

"Well, look who's here," the snotty receptionist said, peering over the top of her glasses. "I don't know if you have heard, but I am afraid Agent Murino is no longer with us. Such a terrible shame," she said, overdramatically clutching her chest.

"Oh yeah, a terrible shame," Peter said, with a bit of condescension in his voice. "We would like to see Chief La Croix, please."

"She's unavailable, but I'll tell her you stopped by."

As the snide employee turned away and began dialing the phone, Peter reached across the counter and hung up the receiver for her.

"Like I was saying, we would like to see Chief La Croix." His tone and pensive facial expression made it abundantly clear that his request was not optional.

"Um, I will call her assistant," the receptionist said, doing an immediate about-face with her attitude. She picked up the phone again, and dialed an internal number. She spoke softly so that Peter and Meredith could not make out exactly what she was saying. But someone on the other end must have taken Peter seriously, because she gave each of them a visitor's pass and sent them up to the seventeenth floor.

"That was incredibly sexy, Peter. I can't tell you how turned on I am right now."

"Really? Well, thank you very much," he said. He straightened his tie, walking with a little swagger down the long hallway.

"Mr. and Mrs. Delaney, Chief La Croix will see you now," a friendly, well-dressed woman said as they approached the reception area.

"Wow, what a difference a few floors makes," Peter whispered.

They were ushered into a huge corner office and offered a beverage. They declined, as they simply wanted to get on with it.

"Hello, Mr. and Mrs. Delaney," Chief La Croix said as she entered the room.

"Thank you so much for seeing us on such short notice. We know you must have a very busy schedule," Meredith said.

"Actually, I called your home thirty minutes ago and left a message on your voice mail."

Meredith and Peter said simultaneously, "You did?"

"Yes. The FBI has become, shall we say, aware of some information that involves you. Can you begin by telling me what you and Agent Murino discussed up until his death?"

They divulged the whole account as succinctly as possible, beginning from the day they first met at the VQ. When they concluded the unbelievable tale, Chief La Croix confided that it is never a good day when an agent is found to have been dishonest in the course of his duties. She sincerely apologized for the months of agony they had endured as a result of Murino's blatant lack of integrity and honor. Two attributes, she went on to say, that are always expected of FBI special agents.

Chief La Croix explained that soon after Agent Murino's murder, the FBI discovered his involvement with Ms. Al-Zarkazi and her associate, the man still only known to the bureau as Simon. The FBI had spent the better part of the week combing through Agent Murino's files, as well as his personal computer. She was able to tell them that Ms. Al-Zarkazi was, indeed, the woman Meredith had seen at the airport, and likely the intruder who had entered their loft while they were away on their honeymoon. She also officially confirmed the connection between Brad Cunningham's murder and Ms. Al-Zarkazi, which caused Peter to wince.

"These details have not yet been released to the public, but we believe it is critical that you both know for security reasons. We are narrowing our search now, and we are confident that we will apprehend them in a matter of hours or days. In the meantime, we would like to put you in a secure location so you will be out of harm's way."

"We would appreciate that, Ms. La Croix. My wife is expecting a baby, and this whole thing has been very upsetting for both of us."

"Well, congratulations. I will have my assistant make the necessary arrangements at the Benson Hotel. Would that be acceptable?"

"Um, sure," Peter said.

Peter and Meredith called their respective employers and told them they had come down with the flu. They were under direct orders to remain silent about the investigation, so claiming an illness was the only plausible way to remain incognito for a few days. The FBI provided each with a bag of toiletries and a change of clothes, immediately bringing a car around to drive them the five short blocks to the hotel.

As the official car pulled up to the main entrance of the hotel, located on Southwest Broadway, the traffic flew by at a fast rate. Meredith stepped up on the curb as Peter exited the vehicle directly into the street. Just as he was about to slam the car door behind him, there were two loud pops, and he fell so quickly Meredith never saw what happened. One agent dove on top of Meredith and the other pulled his weapon, firing at two figures perched above the building across the street. In a matter of seconds the woman who had caused so much pain had fallen five stories to the street below. Next to her lay her accomplice, the man known only as Simon, who had once posed as Peter's college friend in an effort to nick the infamous flash drive that ultimately cost so many people their lives.

Against her will, Meredith was dragged into the lobby of the Benson as the distant sound of sirens descended upon the scene. The driver of their car eventually entered the hotel, and he spotted Meredith immediately. As they locked eyes, she knew without a doubt that Peter was dead. She collapsed on the marble floor, totally inconsolable.

They transported her by ambulance to the closest hospital, which ironically was OHSU, where she had happily visited her father throughout her life. She had not been shot, but they thought it best to examine her since she was pregnant, not to mention the fact that she had been through an incredibly traumatic event.

Dr. Singler was at the hospital at the time, and he was immediately called to the emergency room when the staff learned that his daughter had arrived by ambulance in connection with the shooting at the Benson Hotel. He was at first terrified that Meredith had been shot. Relieved to learn that she was unharmed, he was naturally devastated for her when he learned that Peter was dead. She was released after a thorough examination, and agreed that it was best to go to her parents' home, where she could be taken care of around the clock.

Chapter 14

Meredith did not get out of bed for two days. She remained in her familiar childhood bedroom with the blinds drawn and the lights out, unable to fathom how she would go on without Peter. She was grateful when her parents agreed to handle the funeral arrangements. The service would be held at the same church where Peter and Meredith had been married just a few short months before. And their West Hills home would be more than adequate to accommodate a luncheon following the burial.

"Meredith, I brought you some bouillon. Why don't you sit up and at least try a little. After all, sweetie, you are eating for two now."

Grace Singler had been so excited at the prospect of grandchildren, and was heartbroken that her daughter would not have Peter to share in the joy of watching their child grow up. Over the years, she'd had many friends who had lost husbands to death and divorce, and she was always grateful that she had been blessed with a long and happy marriage. While Meredith was understandably at a low point in her life, Grace was confident in her daughter's inner strength and believed it would eventually emerge, allowing her to find happiness.

The day of the funeral, Meredith showered and put on a black, knee-length Kate Spade dress, a recent splurge at the Nordstrom Anniversary Sale. Her girlfriends had gone to the loft the day before to fetch her things, as it was simply too painful to face the memories that she and Peter had once shared.

The funeral was incredibly sad. In attendance were friends and family. Due to the fact that Peter's death had been profiled in newspapers and on all the cable networks countrywide, the media scoured the street outside the church in hopes of capturing a photograph of the young widow. Luckily, the church made the necessary arrangements, and saw to it that Meredith could duck out the back door in an effort to avoid any unnecessary media attention.

After a long day during which she received an overflowing shower of love and support, she collapsed into bed and cried herself to sleep. She decided not to announce to her friends and colleagues that she was pregnant. She felt it best to wait until she was well into her second trimester. Besides, she was still in denial that she was going to have to embark on motherhood alone. She simply could not believe that just days before, she and Peter had celebrated the news that they would become parents nearly one year to the day that they got married.

Meredith reluctantly returned to the loft after a week. She had decided that she could not hibernate in her parents' home forever, and she would eventually have to return to work. Her boss had been very generous, and told her to take as much time as she needed before returning to the office. Meredith sat in the spacious loft looking at the martini painting over the fireplace. She was tempted to sell it but could not bear to part with the painting that had always been Peter's favorite, even if it had been the inadvertent catalyst of so much deception and pain.

She decided that the first task at hand was to go through the mail. She made herself a cup of tea and took a deep breath, surveying the enormous stack of envelopes that sat before her. She put the bills on the desk, figuring she would pay them later. The junk mail was immediately recycled, and personal notes she put aside because she frankly could not read one more heartfelt card that would cause her to dissolve into tears. She was unsure about a large envelope from their insurance company, though. All they had was a renters policy, and the bill had been paid in full for the year.

She opened it and was shocked to find a copy of an insurance policy, and a check in the sum of two million dollars. At first she thought it was a mistake, but as she read further she realized that Peter had taken the policy out just weeks before his death. She sobbed at the thought, considering the real possibility that he may have had a premonition that his life would be cut short. She immediately picked up the phone and called the insurance agent to inquire further. He gave his condolences, acknowledging that he had seen the article on the front page of the paper and had taken the liberty of processing the payout without first speaking with her. He went on to say that Peter had wanted to make sure she was well taken care of in the event that something happened to him.

Meredith collected her thoughts as best she could, and decided it would be wise to deposit the funds immediately into their bank account. After everything that had happened in the last year, she didn't want to take any chances. She returned home after a quick trip to the bank, and went straight to bed. Between the events of the day and first trimester exhaustion, she could not stay awake any longer.

She woke thinking of Peter. She reached over and touched his pillow. It still smelled like him. She could not believe Peter had the forethought to buy life insurance. He always looked out for her, and even now she felt his presence much of the time.

She gazed at the clock. It was nearly noon, and she had her first ultrasound later that day. Arriving at the doctor's office was bittersweet. So many happy couples, and Meredith sat there by herself. Her parents had offered to go with her, but she'd refused. While she appreciated their support, she somehow felt the need to do this on her own. As she sat in the exam room waiting for her obstetrician, the loneliness was palpable. She had absolutely no clue how she was going to survive by herself.

Her doctor spent almost an hour with her and confirmed that she indeed had a very healthy pregnancy thus far. She gave Meredith a prescription for prenatal vitamins, as well as her routine first trimester advice of keeping stress to a minimum. She acknowledged that Meredith had a unique set of circumstances and suggested that she consider grief counseling to help her navigate the pain of losing a spouse. The doctor confided in Meredith that it had been very helpful in her own journey after her husband died the year before from cancer.

"Thank you, Dr. Stevens. I'll think about it." Meredith graciously accepted the card of a local therapist who specialized in grief counseling.

Meredith returned to work two weeks later, but decided to start slow and go back part-time. Her boss was more than happy to accommodate her request. Meredith was as efficient working twenty hours a week than most of his full-time employees. She had such a great eye for promising writers and as a result was one of the most requested editors on staff.

Chapter 15

As Meredith entered her second trimester, she figured it was time to start telling her friends and co-workers. She was not showing at all, but she knew it was only a matter of time. Everyone was thrilled, letting her know that they would support her in any way she needed. She appreciated their kindness, but somehow it only reminded her how alone she felt in life.

Meredith opted to continue living in the loft. After all, she had plenty of room, and she did not have the time or energy to find a new place to live. Besides, she was close to work and had already established her favorite shops and restaurants in the neighborhood. The local merchants adored Meredith and went out of their way to look out for her.

Christmas was especially painful. She simply could not bear the thought of attending any of the annual holiday festivities. However, her parents insisted she spend Christmas Eve with them, and she finally relented. They meant well, but going to sleep that night in her childhood bedroom only reminded Meredith of Peter's death. By noon Christmas day, she had packed her bag and was headed home. She needed to be alone, fearing that she would never be able to move forward. Painful as it was to see their daughter struggle, Dr. and Mrs. Singler gave her plenty of latitude, quietly conveying to Meredith before she left that they were confident she would eventually find her footing.

Meredith had her monthly prenatal appointment the week after Christmas, and was pleased to learn that the baby was developing as expected.

"So, have you called the therapist I suggested?"

"No, I just haven't had time," Meredith said. But as the words spilled out of her mouth, they both knew it was not the truth.

Dr. Stevens smiled and said, "I know it's a big step, Meredith, but it is proven to be a very helpful way to deal with grief. Especially since you have the added pressure of pregnancy. I really think you would like Dr. Gold."

Meredith went home and thought all evening about what her doctor had said. Reluctantly, she called the number on the card, and made an appointment for the following week.

She showed up feeling ambivalent about going to a therapist. She had always been able to pull herself out of depressing phases in her life, but she knew deep down that she was not equipped to deal with the feelings of despair that continued to suffocate her.

"Hi, I'm Meredith Delaney to see Dr. Gold."

"Great," the receptionist said. "Have a seat. She'll be with you in a few minutes."

Meredith spent the better part of the appointment telling Dr. Gold all about Peter and their life together. She actually felt better as the session concluded, even though she had fallen apart several times during the course of the hour.

"Meredith, I really think I can help you. I know it seems impossible from your perspective, but if you choose to come back I am confident we can make progress."

Meredith really liked Dr. Gold, and sensed that she could help her work through her overwhelming feelings of sadness and heartache. She decided to make a standing appointment, Friday afternoons at three o'clock for the foreseeable future. She felt she owed it to herself, as well as to her unborn child, to find some semblance of normalcy before delving into the next phase of her life.

Chapter 16

The weeks passed quickly, and Meredith began to appear more and more like herself again. Naturally she continued to receive an outpouring of love and support from friends and family, which gave her the courage she needed to persevere.

She felt huge, even though she actually remained quite slim, except for a basketball-size pooch. She was impressed by the variety of designers who had thrown their proverbial hats into the ring of maternity wear. While she could not justify purchasing an entire new wardrobe, she had found several outfits that she loved.

As Meredith approached Southwest Stark Street on an uncharacteristically warm and sunny Sunday morning, she heard a chorus of familiar voices behind her. In unison they chanted how incredibly radiant she looked. Meredith turned to see her oldest girlfriends, whom she was meeting at Mother's Bistro for breakfast. It was a fan favorite in Portland, and they loved the atmosphere.

"Thanks, you guys. I am feeling good. And I have news," she said, smiling in a way they had not seen in months.

They were seated almost immediately in the corner, directly under a gigantic chandelier dripping with crystals and antique beads. They all looked at her wide-eyed, waiting with bated breath for the impending announcement.

"I finally decided to find out, and." She paused. "It's a girl!"

The table of eight simultaneously screamed, causing everyone in the restaurant to look over. They didn't care, and continued to celebrate the terrific news by toasting with steaming mugs of the ever-popular Stumptown coffee.

Her dearest childhood friend said, "Have you decided on a name, Mer?"

"No. I think I'm going to wait and meet her first."

Brunch was just like old times, and they were thrilled to see that their friend was starting to come back to them after such an arduous year. Each took the time to share with Meredith how proud they were of her strength and resilience since Peter's death.

The final weeks of Meredith's pregnancy were quickly descending upon her, and she spent them completing the nursery and reading books, including the ever-popular *What to Expect When You're Expecting*. Her parents visited often, reminding her that they were there to help in any way she needed. They could see that their daughter was feeling much stronger, and they smiled broadly as Meredith credited her newfound confidence to the weeks spent with her grief counselor.

In her thirty-ninth week Meredith lay in bed, making a mental note of last-minute tasks she needed to tend to the following day. Unsure if she was awake or asleep, she had a vision so vivid it caused her to sit up in a cold sweat. She still dreamed of Peter often, but this was different. He stood at the foot of her bed, conveying to Meredith how much he loved her. He went on to say how proud he was of her bravery, and that he could not wait to watch over Poppy as she grew up.

The apparition dissolved, almost into thin air. As Meredith stood up, to collect her thoughts and make yet another trip to the bathroom, her water broke. In a moment of panic she stood paralyzed, not knowing what to do. She finally made her way to the phone and called her mother, who had told her that she would be available to drive her to the hospital day or night. In a matter of minutes both Dr. and Mrs. Singler were at Meredith's front door. With very little nighttime traffic, they easily pulled directly in front of the entrance to St. Vincent hospital with plenty of time to spare.

Meredith was a trooper. She was in labor for almost twelve hours and gave birth in a matter of minutes. The newborn was healthy, weighing in at just over seven pounds. Not wasting a moment, the pink bundle immediately began squalling, to laughter and applause from Portland's newest grandparents. While Meredith knew she would one day reflect back and remember the birth of her daughter as a magical day, she was still heartbroken, welling up at the fleeting thought that Peter was not there to share it with her.

Later that day the nurse came in to help Meredith nurse the baby, and asked if she had decided on a name.

"Poppy," Meredith said. "Poppy Delaney."

"That is such a sweet name. I'm not sure we have ever had a Poppy at St. Vincent. Is it a family name?"

"No, it reminds me of a special memory that I shared with my husband on our honeymoon," Meredith whispered, as she stared into the huge blue eyes of her baby girl.

The nurse did not question her further, as the staff had all been forewarned of Meredith's devastating situation.

Two days later Meredith and Poppy were released from the hospital. Dr. and Mrs. Singler begged her to come home with them, but she refused. She wanted to become better acquainted with Miss Poppy in the quiet confines of her loft. And after her experience the night before Poppy's birth, she wanted the energy in her daughter's first days to be as peaceful and relaxed as possible.

Poppy was a fantastic baby. She slept and nursed well, and was growing like crazy. Meredith, of course, could not help but dress her up, proudly beaming when strangers stopped her to compliment Poppy's big blue eyes and happy demeanor.

The week before Meredith was scheduled to go back to work, her boss called and asked her to have coffee. They met downstairs at the French cafe, and Poppy happily slept in her stroller while they talked.

"I don't know if it's too soon, Meredith, but I really think you should write a book."

"A book?"

"Now, hear me out," he said, putting his hands up as if to reject her bemused expression. "You are one of the most talented writers I have ever come across, and I think, when you're ready, you should write about your experience last year."

Meredith had come so far in such a short period of time. Just a few months before, the conversation would have brought her to tears. She was, at least, now in a place where she could make reference to Peter. However, she was not sure she would ever be ready to rehash the events of his death in written form.

"Thank you for your confidence in my abilities. Tell you what, I will agree to, at least, give it some thought."

Meredith went to bed that night missing Peter. Every time she entered the familiar loft, she was reminded that he would never walk through the door to greet his family. But as quickly as the thoughts of sadness emerged, she reminded herself that she had been given the gift of a beautiful, healthy baby, who looked exactly like her father when she smiled.

That night the loft was especially quiet, and Meredith lay in bed appreciating the silence. Feeling the familiar presence of Peter's spirit descend upon the room, she had no doubt that she was fully awake, and was experiencing more than the illusion of her husband.

"Mer, it is time for you to move on. You are always going to feel stagnant if you stay in Portland. You and Poppy are meant to move to Larkspur. You will have a beautiful life in Marin County, and I will always be with you."

As quickly as Peter had appeared, he was gone, leaving Meredith numb and blindsided by the suggestion that a massive life change would result in a sanguine conclusion.

Chapter 17

With three days left before Meredith was scheduled to go back to work, she sat down and Googled Larkspur, California. The photos that popped up on the monitor brought tears to her eyes. She was instantly reminded of the quaint town where she and Peter had stopped for lunch on their way to Sonoma. She recalled falling in love with everything from the people to the terrific energy of the community. The weather was a draw, as well. Sunny with a marine breeze. She could certainly get used to that, she thought.

"This is crazy," she said out loud. And just as she said it, she spontaneously clicked on the picture of a bungalow for rent. It was a charming two-bedroom, surrounded by a white picket fence. The short walk to town, not to mention the spectacular cook's kitchen, piqued Meredith's interest.

She could not believe she was doing it, but before she could stop herself, she sent a note to the property manager inquiring about its availability. Meredith went to bed dreaming about the Bay Area. At the very least, it was a nice diversion at a time when she was feeling melancholy about the prospect of staying in a city that constantly reminded her of the past.

The next morning Meredith woke to a blustery rainy day. She lit a fire in the fireplace, and nestled in with Poppy. She felt like her little girl was the one element in her life that allowed her to function normally. She smiled at the cooing baby, thinking to herself that she could gaze into her big blue eyes all day long.

At noon she fed Poppy, then put her down for a nap. Meredith decided to check her emails, and among them was a response from the property manager in Larkspur. Apparently, another couple had been interested, but recently backed out. The property manager warned that rentals typically went quickly in Marin, and while the property had become available again, the charming house would surely be snatched up within the week. Meredith thought about her visit from Peter and began feeling like a move might be a good thing for her.

The next day she asked her boss to meet her for coffee again. He thought for sure she was going to agree to write the book that they had discussed in their previous meeting. Naturally, he was shocked when she told him that she was moving to California.

Meredith could see that he was already thinking about how he was going to replace her, and she said in an uncharacteristically flinty tone, "I will agree to write a book, but not the one we talked about the other day. Frankly, I don't know if I will ever be able to rehash the events of last year. But I have some ideas about a fictional series that have been rattling around in my head. Of course I would love for you to be my publisher, if you are interested."

He listened to her ideas and was instantly intrigued. "Meredith, I am sad to lose you as an editor, but thrilled to gain you as a client."

As Meredith walked home, she giggled to herself. "I cannot believe I'm doing this," she said under her breath. But deep down she felt it was the right decision, and she truly believed Peter's guidance was going to help her navigate her way. It was the first time in a long time that Meredith had genuinely felt excited about her future. Now she would have to tell her parents, which was going to be a tough conversation.

The announcement went better than Meredith expected. Her parents clearly wanted the best for their daughter, and they could tell that she was happier, looking more and more like the Meredith they had always known and loved. As she told them about the charming town, they both noticed that it was the first time since Peter's death that she seemed encouraged about the next chapter in her life.

"Well, be prepared for frequent visits, because we don't want to miss this little one growing up." As always, both Dr. and Mrs. Singler were transfixed by Poppy, taking turns nuzzling her neck until she squealed with glee.

Meredith returned home that afternoon and went immediately into organization mode. She had decided to hire a moving company but wanted to discard items that she had never really liked and would not need in her new home.

The following week, she was relieved when the Goodwill truck finally pulled away, leaving only the belongings she deemed necessary. The movers were scheduled to be there first thing the next morning. Everything was happening so quickly, but for some reason the details seemed to be falling into place with great ease. She could almost feel herself being taken by the hand and led down the right path. And there was no question in her mind that Peter was the one quietly clearing the way for her to discover her destiny.

That night Meredith and her pals gathered at Huber's Cafe for a final send-off, commemorating years of love and friendship with a customary round of Spanish coffees. She rarely left Poppy but felt comfortable entrusting the baby to her parents for the evening. They were more than happy to take advantage of the last moments with their granddaughter before the big move to California.

"To Meredith." Her friends simultaneously raised their glasses, making every effort to choke back their sadness. While they could tell Meredith was in a much better place, none of her friends could wrap their heads around why she would choose to move to a town where she did not know a single soul.

After many tearful goodbyes, Meredith and Poppy departed in the SUV that Meredith had purchased the week before. She'd never had any need for a car, since she and Peter had lived and worked in downtown Portland. But her life was definitely changing now, and Meredith knew she would need a reliable vehicle to get around Marin.

Poppy, secured in her car seat, fell asleep as soon as they hit I-5. They stopped in Ashland and stayed at the historic Ashland Springs Hotel for the night. The last time Meredith visited Ashland was in high school, to attend the Shakespeare Festival with her parents. The area remained unchanged, still the charming yet sophisticated little town, nestled in the mountains of southern Oregon, that she remembered from ten years before. After a quick supper Meredith and Poppy fell into bed, to rest for the long day of driving that lay ahead.

Meredith was mesmerized by the spectacular grandeur of Mount Shasta and could feel the anticipation of her new adventure as she finally reached Sonoma. It was unfathomable to her that she would actually be able to spend the day in wine country or San Francisco with little to no effort. And as she finally merged onto Highway 101, and saw the sign that read "Welcome to Marin County," she shed tears of joy, knowing she had made the right decision.

"We're home, Poppy," Meredith whispered to the sleeping baby.

Chapter 18

*I*t was a perfectly sunny day with a hint of a breeze, and Meredith easily found the property manager's office. In a matter of minutes, she wrote a check and signed the lease. Just like that, Meredith and Poppy were proud residents of Larkspur, California.

As they walked to their car, Meredith sang in a silly way, "Poppy, Poppy, Poppy, we're California girls now. It's time to turn our rain boots in for flip-flops!" Poppy smiled whenever her mom said anything, and this caused her to let out a huge squeal.

They pulled into the driveway and the whole thing became very real, very fast. Meredith whispered, "Peter, please let me know I have done the right thing."

She kissed the top of Poppy's head as she pulled the infant from her seat, and jockeyed to unlock the front door. She entered the foyer and stood still, surveying the place. She did not know why, but she felt a sense of peace and tranquility. Walking through the living room and into the sunny kitchen, she was taken aback when she saw a small silver vase containing three red poppies on the marble countertop. The arrangement looked exactly like the red poppies in the painting Peter had given her as a gift on their honeymoon.

"Who could have possibly done this?" she whispered. The only person she'd spoken with was the property manager, and they had never discussed anything except the specifics of the house and where the rent was to be paid. She had never even made reference to her daughter's name in the course of their discussions.

"Thank you, Peter," Meredith said, as tears sprung from her eyes. She knew it was some greater power letting her know she was doing the right thing. And with that, she took a deep breath, and unloaded the car while Poppy snoozed happily in her travel crib.

The moving truck was scheduled to arrive later that afternoon, so Meredith took the opportunity to make a quick trip to Trader Joe's and Whole Foods to stock the pantry and refrigerator. She could not wait to test her culinary skills out on the Wolf range. Meredith had cooked and baked since childhood but had never before had the privilege of chef's-grade appliances.

The movers rang the doorbell at four o'clock sharp, and within two hours the truck was empty. They were so efficient that it seemed like everything was in place in no time. Meredith tipped them generously, as everything had arrived in perfect condition.

Poppy went to sleep early, and Meredith took the opportunity to continue unpacking even though she was utterly exhausted. As she made up her bed, she felt totally at home. The house was warm and cozy, and she knew in her heart that Larkspur was going to be a good place to raise her daughter.

They both slept in the next day, and after a pot of coffee Meredith finished putting the nursery together. By ten o'clock Meredith was famished and anxious to rediscover Larkspur, so she and Poppy walked into town for a late breakfast. They ended their stroll at Rulli's, the charming Italian cafe where Peter and Meredith had lunched while on their honeymoon. Meredith sat with Poppy outside, lazily people-watching and scanning the *Marin Independent Journal* to become acquainted with local news and events. She was especially interested in a story about Kathryn Cahill, a local woman who had started a nonprofit organization to rescue homeless animals. She primarily saved dogs and cats, but it was not uncommon for her to save the likes of bunnies, chickens, and the occasional horse.

That afternoon, while Miss Poppy took a nap in the shade of the backyard trees, Meredith took a closer look at the small structure located in the garden behind the house. It occurred to her that it would make an excellent office and art studio. The once single-car garage had received a respectable facelift the prior year when the kitchen was remodeled. The lighting was fantastic, and the previous owners had added French doors to replicate the grand floor-to-ceiling windows that extended across the back of the house.

"First order of business," Meredith said out loud, "is to find an art store."

"There's a great one in Corte Madera," a voice chirped from over the fence.

Meredith jumped. "Um, hello?"

A red head popped up over the top of the fence. "Sorry to startle you. I'm Kathryn Cahill. I live next door. I didn't mean to eavesdrop, but I couldn't help but hear you talking about needing art supplies."

"Hi, I'm Meredith Delaney, and this little squirt in the bassinet is my daughter, Poppy."

"Welcome, Meredith. You can't miss it. It's the best art store in Marin, and is located right between Nordstrom and Anthropologie."

"Kathryn, did I just read an article about you in the local paper?"

"Guilty as charged. Can I interest you in a dog?" she said, without missing a beat.

"I'll get back to you on that one. I've got my hands full at the moment."

Meredith chuckled as Kathryn gave her a wave goodbye. She could tell she was really going to like her. She noticed that Kathryn was not wearing a wedding ring and could not help but wonder about her back story. The article had spoken very highly of her; she was obviously a rock star in Marin, judging from the way she'd been portrayed in the paper.

Poppy woke up happy and rested. Meredith got cleaned up and decided to venture out for art supplies. With Kathryn's directions in hand, she found the store without too much trouble.

"Wow," Meredith said as she entered. "I feel like a kid in a candy store, Poppy."

"Can I help you?" an older gentleman said.

"I need some basics for a small art studio I am putting together."

After less than an hour, Meredith stood back while a slew of employees filled the back of her car with everything she would need to set up a studio. She also purchased a work table that could easily be used for writing, which the store was more than happy to deliver the following morning. She was excited to get home and put everything in its proper place. It had been a long time since Meredith had expressed her artistic side, and she was thrilled that her creative energy was finally beginning to emerge after lying dormant for nearly a year. There was almost a magical feeling to the funky little town of Larkspur, and Meredith had a sneaking suspicion that she was meant to do something special. She did not know exactly what, but she had an inkling that she was being ushered to greatness by a force far greater than her own.

Chapter 19

The first month flew by, and Meredith could not believe how well she had acclimated to living alone in a new town. As she puttered around the house one evening, the phone rang.

"Hey neighbor, it's Kathryn Cahill. So are you still living out of boxes?"

"Hi, Kathryn, we are all settled and loving Larkspur!"

"It's tough not to fall in love with the Bay Area. I have lived here my whole life, and I never plan on leaving. I was wondering if you wanted to have coffee sometime."

"What are you doing right now? Poppy is already sleeping. I could make some coffee or open a bottle of wine."

"Wine sounds great! Be right over."

Meredith greeted her with a hug. Kathryn was an interesting gal, sporting a pair of faded jeans, four-inch platforms, and a J.Crew animal-print cardigan slung casually over her shoulders. In her hair, which was cut in a severe chin-length bob, was a huge turquoise flower clip. Somehow, she managed to pull off the eclectic look with unbelievable style, a cross between a grown-up version of Scout from *To Kill a Mockingbird* and Vogue's chic editor-in-chief. Regardless, Meredith liked her warm personality and felt certain they could become good friends.

"I love what you've done with the place, Mer. Can I call you Mer?"

It caught Meredith off guard a bit, as Peter had always called her by that name. She quietly acknowledged the fleeting memory, while remaining upbeat so as not to create an awkward moment over something as harmless as a nickname. "Sure."

"This martini painting is spectacular. Who's the artist?"

"That's one of mine."

"You are sure in the right place. Marin is swarming with artists, musicians, actors; you name a celeb, and they most likely have a house in the area."

"Have a seat. I opened a bottle of pinot, but I have chardonnay if you prefer."

"Pinot's great. So, do you sell your art locally?"

"No, it's really just a hobby. I am actually a writer. Well, I was an editor after college, but I am planning to take a stab at writing a series."

"Wow, Mer. That's great! Where'd you go to college?"

"Stanford."

"Really. I went to Cal."

"So, tell me more about your nonprofit," Meredith said, putting down a tray of crudités and other nibbles.

"I have always had a soft spot for animals. I cannot tell you how many dogs I have risked my life for on the side of the road. It never ceases to amaze me when people just toss their pet aside like garbage simply because they don't want to care for it any longer. So, long story short, I decided to do something about it."

"That's awesome."

"In fact, we are having a swanky black-tie benefit in a few months. You should come," Kathryn chirped, piling veggies onto her plate.

"A black-tie event for animals?" Meredith said with a giggle.

"I know it sounds kind of crazy, but last year we had over a thousand people and raised almost a million dollars."

"Are you serious?" Meredith said, almost spitting her wine out. "It's official; I'm definitely not fancy enough to live here, Kathryn!"

Kathryn laughed. "I know what you mean, Mer. You'll get used to it, though. There's a ton of money, and more liberals per capita than an MSNBC office party. That combination means cha-ching for my nonprofit." And with that, they toasted, and finished the bottle.

Meredith laughed out loud as she locked the door after saying goodbye to her new friend. She had learned that Kathryn grew up in the neighboring town of Ross and attended Branson, a very expensive and highly regarded private high school that attracted the brightest and most elite Marin students.

"So, who are you, Kathryn Cahill," she curiously said out loud, pulling out her iPad to Google her quirky neighbor. Her mouth dropped open as hundreds of photos and websites popped up.

"Holy crap, you're the daughter of Senator Claire Cahill?" Meredith said, as if questioning the screen in front of her.

It all made sense. The impervious Claire Cahill was one of Washington, D.C.'s most beloved politicians, and had been for nearly twenty years. More recently, she had become known for her work supporting the rights of women in the military. In fact, Meredith recalled reading an article in the *New York Times* the previous month that chronicled the rampant sexual abuse involving thousands of servicemen and women each year. It was none other than Senator Cahill who was responsible for introducing a bill demanding a change in the way investigations were conducted into sexual assaults by fellow soldiers. High-ranking officers were discovered to have been derelict in their duties, failing time and time again to hold perpetrators responsible for their criminal actions. The unfortunate pattern eventually found its way into the public forum and generated an outcry from American citizens. The article had essentially hailed Cahill as a warrior for standing before her colleagues on the Senate floor and delivering what was said to be the most inspirational and powerful speech of the decade—a speech that implored those in the room to vote to protect the nation's unsung heroes. The article went on to say that the support that she gleaned from both sides of the aisle was unprecedented, and would surely put her in line to, at least, engage in a conversation about an impending run for the White House.

"I feel so stupid," Meredith said, dropping her head in her hands.

That night she fell asleep trying to decide if she should say anything about her inadvertent faux pas. She ultimately opted not to make a big deal of the failed connection. After all, she genuinely liked Kathryn, and did not want her to think she was trying to get chummy because of her high-profile family.

Chapter 20

The next day, when the phone rang, Meredith picked it up and was surprised to hear a familiar voice. "So how much have you written, Meredith?"

"Hey, Spencer. Great to hear from you!"

Spencer had once occupied the office next to Meredith's, and he'd assumed responsibility of her pending manuscripts when she moved to California. He had also been assigned to edit Meredith's first book, which he was fully confident would eventually evolve into a successful series.

"I've got it all in my head, but nothing on the computer yet. I have been kind of distracted by the glow of the California sun," Meredith said, in a way she knew would make him crazy with envy.

"Thanks a lot, Meredith. It has rained for nine days straight, and there doesn't seem to be an end to it for the foreseeable future."

"So, what's going on in Portland, besides the rain?"

"Not much. Oh, but you know that hot yoga guy from Sellwood we were vying for?"

"Hot yoga guy?"

"You know, he wrote that book on vegan living?"

"Oh yeah, I remember."

"We finally negotiated a sweet deal with him to write a three-part series on the health benefits of mindful meditation, thank you very much."

"Nice."

"Better than nice, Mer. Don't get me wrong. I have no intention of eating his Styrofoam food and sweating like a dog in his hippie kumbaya class, but his books are the reason I will be lying on the beach in Maui for two weeks this year!"

"Sounds like you're doing well, Spence. How's everything with Annie?"

"We broke up. Know any beautiful California girls?"

"Not really. Although I just found out that my next-door neighbor is the daughter of Senator Claire Cahill."

"Well, hello there fancy pants! No wonder you haven't written anything yet. You've been schmoozing with the beautiful people."

"The what?"

"You know, Meredith, the beautiful people. The rich, attractive movers and shakers that live off trust funds and relieve their silver spoon guilt by periodically volunteering at a soup kitchen. From what I hear, Marin County is crawling with them!"

"I have no clue, Spencer. You know me, I always fly under the radar when it comes to social climbing. All I know is that Kathryn Cahill is really nice. She runs a nonprofit for animals, after all! I'm pretty sure she's the real deal, Spence."

"Is she cute, Mer?"

"She's not your type."

"What are you talking about? Everybody's my type!"

"Well, let's just say she's the type who would happily sprint to hot yoga and top off the day with a vegan delicacy from what's-his-name's book."

"Touché. So, when can I expect to read your first few chapters?"

"Give me a month?"

"Done. Talk to you later, Mer."

Meredith hung up the phone, laughing to herself. She had given her series a great deal of thought and figured she should at least outline the main premise, as well as the first few chapters. She sat down at her kitchen table after tucking Poppy into bed and flipped open her laptop. Before she knew it, four hours had passed, and it was well after midnight. Scanning the loose synopsis of book number one, Meredith was more than pleased to find that she had produced a promising summary with a rich group of characters.

At six o'clock sharp Poppy began babbling from her crib, though she was perfectly happy to snuggle in bed with Meredith, both snoozing on and off for another hour. Poppy was nearly six months old and was rapidly developing the most hilarious personality. Every day she did little things that reminded Meredith of Peter. The night before, she had been visibly annoyed when Meredith took away a knife that Poppy was attempting to grab from the dinner table. The angry pout that she'd produced made Meredith laugh out loud. She looked at the frustrated tot, affectionately saying, "My dear, you look exactly like your daddy right now." It tugged at her heart, but she felt enormously grateful to have a wonderful reminder of the man she would always love.

That afternoon during Poppy's nap, Meredith went through some photo albums that she'd pushed to the back closet when they moved in. She came across their wedding album and could not resist. It had been such a beautiful day, followed by an equally magical honeymoon. As she reminisced alone on the floor of the bungalow, she dissolved into tears at the thought of everything she had lost. The last two years still seemed like a strange nightmare, often causing her to believe she might one day wake up and tell Peter the terrifying details over coffee. As quickly as she'd pulled the albums out, she returned them to their box, tucking them away for another time. Splashing cold water on her face, Meredith decided that she could only handle baby steps. There would never be anyone who could compare to Peter. At the very least, she reminded herself, she had experienced love once, if only for a short time.

Chapter 21

$\mathcal{M}$eredith managed to churn out three chapters in a relatively short period of time. She immediately sent them to Spencer, hoping he would be equally pleased with the direction she was taking.

"Let's take a walk to Rulli's, Miss Poppy. Your mom is very tired today and could really use a latte and some fresh air."

As they strolled down Magnolia Street, they ran into Kathryn, who was having coffee with an exceptionally handsome man at one of the outside tables. She introduced Meredith but did not ask her to join them. Meredith figured he was a business associate, as Kathryn was wearing a wrap dress and incredibly cute Tory Burch flats. She had not seen Kathryn in anything but shorts or denim and could not get over how sophisticated she looked. She definitely seemed a little nervous, Meredith thought. She remembered that Kathryn's foundation was planning a huge black-tie affair the following month and suspected that the last-minute details were causing her some stress. As a result, Meredith decided to sit inside so as to not be a distraction. Poppy had recently developed the adorable but very loud habit of squealing every time a dog passed by, and she did not want to escalate an already tense situation.

Later that day there was a knock at the door. Meredith quickly answered it so Poppy would not prematurely wake from her much-needed nap.

"Hey Mer, I want to apologize for this morning," Kathryn said.

"Come in, come in. Lemonade?"

"Sure."

They sat outside in the shade. Kathryn had not seen the art studio since Meredith filled it with supplies, and she was totally blown away.

"Mer, I love the studio."

"Thanks. The light is perfect, and I'm close enough to hear Poppy when she is napping. It's a win-win."

Getting back to the reason she came over, Kathryn said, "I feel absolutely horrible about how rude I was this morning. I swear this event is going to put me in an early grave."

"What's going on?"

"Well, I depend on private donors to underwrite the event itself. That way, all the donations raised during the course of the evening go directly to the foundation. The guy I was meeting with this morning advised me that his company was pulling their hundred-thousand-dollar pledge, which puts us in a predicament unless I can find another donor fast."

"Funnily enough, Kathryn, I know someone who might be in a position to help."

"You do? Who?"

"Well, there would, of course, be conditions," Meredith said with a cagey smirk.

"What kind of conditions?" Kathryn said, with a suspicious raise of the eyebrow.

"The next time you hear of a rescue Labradoodle, it's mine!"

"You're the donor?"

Meredith nonchalantly inspected her manicure, as if she had just offered to loan Kathryn something as insignificant as a cup of sugar.

"Meredith, this is a very generous offer. I certainly don't want to pry, but a hundred grand is a sizable amount of money."

"Kathryn, I really like you, and I feel like I should be straight with you. I was married to the greatest guy in the world. Unfortunately, we had a friend who was in bed with a dirty FBI agent, and . . ."

"Wait, are you talking about that huge al-Qaeda case last year in Portland?"

Meredith nodded. It was still so raw after a year that she rarely brought the subject up. Tears came into her eyes, as always when she spoke of Peter, but she was able to pull herself together quickly.

"Oh my god, Mer. I am so sorry. I had no idea!"

"How could you, Kathryn? So, I would like to donate one hundred thousand dollars." She wiped a single tear from her cheek with the back of her hand. "My husband, Peter, must have had a premonition or something, because he saw to it that Poppy and I would be well taken care of in the event of his death."

At this point Kathryn was almost sobbing at the thought of Meredith's insurmountable loss, as well as her selfless generosity. "This means so much to me, Mer. And to the foundation, as well."

In an effort to lighten the mood, Meredith said, "Well, I'd better not be seated next to the kitchen."

They both laughed, and Kathryn gave her friend a hug before she left. "Thanks, Mer."

"Yeah, I'm holding you to that Labradoodle, too!"

"Got it!" And with that Kathryn almost skipped home.

Just as Meredith sat down to enjoy her afternoon green tea, the phone rang. "Hey, sweetie. It's mom. Your dad and I would like to plan a visit next month. Is that a good time for you?"

The two chatted for almost an hour, and when Meredith hung up she was relieved. Her parents were more than happy to plan their trip around Kathryn's event, and equally thrilled to babysit Poppy while Meredith took a well-deserved night off to socialize with Marin County's movers and shakers.

As Meredith got into bed, it occurred to her that she would need a dress for the elaborate occasion. Maybe she would take the baby into the city the next day, for a little retail therapy and a brisk walk along the water. She smiled as she replayed the events of the day and fell asleep knowing that Peter would have approved of her generous donation. In fact, he would have done exactly the same if the tables were turned.

Chapter 22

The following day Poppy woke with the sniffles so Meredith decided to put off going into San Francisco until her little one felt better. It was just as well, because Spencer called, hoping to discuss the preliminary outline and chapters she had emailed to him the previous week.

"Mer, it's awesome! We discussed it during our morning meeting, and it was unanimous. We are on board. You should anticipate a FedEx with a formal contract on your doorstep later this week."

"Seriously, Spence? Any changes or suggestions?"

"Nope, we all love it as is. So, how soon can we see more? Our goal is to get it into bookstores and on every possible website in time for the holidays."

"What? Spencer, that doesn't give me much time."

"Sounds like you'd better get off your lounge chair, put your umbrella drink down, and get to work," Spencer said, and gave an evil laugh.

"Okay, okay, I get it. You're cranky because you haven't seen the sun in weeks."

"That's not entirely true. Today there was the hint of the outline of the sun behind a dark cloud."

"Poor thing. I'll see what I can do, Spencer. I have to go now. Poppy has a cold, and I think I hear her fussing."

"Talk to you soon, Mer. Oh, by the way, nice job. You should be really proud of yourself."

Meredith hung up and danced around like a schoolgirl. She could feel Peter around her all the time, and she knew it was his hand quietly guiding her down a new path.

Within a few days Poppy was better, so Meredith took the opportunity to zip into the city to look at dresses for the upcoming benefit. She wanted to be comfortable, but she also figured it would be fun to wear something chic and kind of sexy. She began her search at Neiman Marcus, which was bittersweet. The last time she'd shopped in San Francisco was during their honeymoon, and Meredith smiled at the memory of Peter's insistence that she treat herself to a dress at the upscale clothing store. The renowned four-story rotunda sitting prominently on Union Square was a draw for locals and visitors alike. Meredith made a mental note to return during the holidays to admire the floor-to-ceiling Christmas tree that filled the elaborate foyer each year.

The ladies in the formal dress department, all well aware of the annual charity event, told Meredith that she should definitely wear a full-length gown. After all, they said, the men would all be in tuxedos, and the women wouldn't be caught dead in a simple cocktail dress. They acted as if it would be an indisputable crime to wear anything less than customary formal attire. One snooty salesperson even whispered to Meredith, with a Cape-Coddy kind of inflection, "It's kind of a big shindig because Senator Cahill always attends. You know, her daughter is the one who runs the nonprofit organization, so all the Bay Area celebrities and political heavy hitters will be there. Really, everybody who's anybody, dear."

"I see," Meredith said, trying to give the illusion of actually caring. She had no intention of dishing malicious gossip or disclosing that she and Kathryn were neighbors. As she closed the door to the dressing room, Meredith rolled her eyes, recalling that Peter used to jokingly refer to the high-end store as "Needless Markup."

Meredith eventually found the perfect dress and a pair of stunningly high heels that made her nearly six feet tall. When she emerged from the dressing room, all eyes were upon her. She looked spectacular as she examined herself in the three-way mirror that stood prominently in the center of the dress department. A series of claps from Poppy sealed it, giving everyone a good laugh. And with that, Meredith left the store with an ensemble that could have easily made any best-dressed list.

On the way home, Meredith and Poppy stopped off at the marina and took a brisk walk down the familiar pathway that paralleled the bay. It had turned out to be quite a day of remembrances. First shopping in the city, followed by the beautiful stroll to Crissy Field. They concluded their outing at the Warming Hut. Meredith bought herself a cup of tea, as well as a lemon scone that she and Poppy shared while sitting on the same rock wall on which she and Peter had perched a little over a year ago. The sun was warm, and their attention soon turned to a group of seals playing in the waves. While difficult, it had turned out to be a lovely day, and they headed home for a quiet evening.

Chapter 23

First thing in the morning Meredith found a FedEx envelope on her doorstep. It was the contract formally outlining the verbal agreement that had been solidified prior to Meredith's move to Larkspur. The lengthy document confirmed a three-book series to be published over the course of five years. Meredith felt confident that she could easily produce a book every eighteen months. The offer was more than generous, and the series had the potential to become even more lucrative if it ultimately reached the *New York Times* best-seller list. However, true to Meredith's unconventional style, she did not give the final rewards much consideration. Like her father, she believed that if she prematurely focused on the prize, it would surely cause her to take her eye off the proverbial ball.

Meredith thought it best to have a lawyer review the documents prior to signing. She mentioned this to Kathryn, who highly recommended her personal attorney. She was known for being one of the toughest negotiators around, with a stellar reputation among her Bay Area colleagues.

"So, all ready for the big party next week?"

"Yes, but this year has been especially challenging. We are at a record twelve hundred, which is great, but it's quite an undertaking at the same time."

"Please tell me I am sitting with fun people, Kathryn."

"Are you kidding? You're at my table. You don't think I'd stick you with a bunch of fuddy-duddies, do you?"

"Well, I should hope not! Honestly, I am mostly looking forward to an evening off of mommy duty. My parents will be in town, so I can party all night if I want to," Meredith said with a glimmer in her eye.

"Don't worry, Mer. Once the auction concludes, the real party begins! Oh, that reminds me, I have to buzz down to Sausalito to pick up the final auction catalogs from the printer. Would you and Poppy like to keep me company, and join me for lunch today?"

"Um, sure."

"Have you ever been to Fish?"

"Fish?"

"Oh my gosh, Mer, best seafood in Marin. Right on the water. You'll love it!"

"Sounds great!"

"Okay, I am going for a quick run, but I'll be ready to go around noon."

Meredith was able to spend a few hours working on her book while Poppy napped. She promised herself she would write for three hours a day so she could easily make her deadline. She was not too worried, but, being a perfectionist, she wanted the final product to be impeccable.

Kathryn was right. Fish was a huge hit. They both scarfed down an order of fish tacos, with a huge family-style salad to share. Poppy was perfectly content watching the seagulls while Meredith and Kathryn happily chatted on the sunny deck.

"I'll be right back, Kathryn," Meredith said, scooping the tot up from her high chair. She wanted to fetch Poppy some milk for the ride home, and as she rounded the corner, she came face to face with another customer.

"Oh, I'm sorry," Meredith said; she'd almost run smack into him.

"I'm not," he said, smiling. "Who's this?"

"This is Poppy."

"Well, hello there, Poppy."

Meredith's little flirt wrinkled up her nose and squealed, showing off a new tooth that was trying to push its way up.

"She's adorable. Hi, I'm Alan Harrison."

Meredith did not know what was happening to her, but she suddenly felt warm and dizzy. When they shook hands it was as if an electric current shot right through her. She was so thrown by the introduction that she said a quick goodbye, abandoning the milk and making a beeline for the car. She wasn't even sure she'd told him her name.

As she awkwardly buckled Poppy into her infant seat, Kathryn casually said, "Was that Alan I saw you talking to? I didn't know you knew each other."

"You know him?" Meredith said.

"Meredith, everyone knows him. He's an award-winning screenwriter. If you saw the Oscars last year, he took home the Academy Award for best picture."

Meredith had no recollection of the prior year. She had spent much of it mourning the death of her husband and doing everything in her power to be the best mother she could be.

"I don't know him. Although I just about knocked him over." After that, Meredith changed the subject. She felt incredibly guilty, even though she knew she had nothing to feel guilty about. Why was she so disarmed by this man? They had instantaneously locked eyes, resulting in Meredith's inability to string a sentence together.

That night after Poppy went to bed, Meredith continued to replay the events of the day. It never occurred to her that she would ever meet anyone even remotely as special as Peter, but she could not deny that there had been an immediate connection with Alan Harrison.

Meredith awoke just after midnight and was unable to fall back asleep. She often felt Peter's energy in the room, but it had been a while since he visited her in a dream. Just as Meredith began dozing off, she felt his presence with more clarity than ever before. She became transfixed as his image appeared near the foot of the bed, speaking to her with the familiar cadence that she had always loved.

"Mer, it is time for you to move forward. You are a wonderful mother, and you have a great future ahead of you as a writer. I want you to know that I will always love you and watch out for both you and Poppy. Trust your instincts, and know that it is okay for you to have a life of happiness."

Meredith did not know exactly what that meant, but tears spilled onto her pillow as she felt Peter's presence vanish. It was almost as if Peter were saying his final goodbyes, after being spiritually tethered to Meredith for the better part of a year. In her heart she knew that from that moment on, she was on her own.

Chapter 24

wo days later, Meredith's parents arrived. They opted to stay at a local hotel, since Meredith's bungalow was small and did not have a proper guest room. They could not believe how big Poppy had gotten and were beyond thrilled to see how well their daughter had acclimated to her new environment. Before their arrival, they had not been so sure about her choice to leave Portland and her lifelong network of family and friends. But it was not long before they were convinced she had made an excellent decision to begin a new life in the Bay Area. Meredith had made a remarkable transformation, and it gave her parents great pride to observe how far she had come in such a short period of time.

"Let's walk down to the Lark Creek Inn for dinner this evening. We can sit on the deck and get a bottle of wine. Sound good?"

"Sounds great, sweetie. I just want you to know that Dad and I are simply thrilled to be with you and Miss Poppy for the week." And with that, Meredith's mother gave her daughter a huge hug.

The Lark Creek Inn was a Bay Area favorite. The grand fireplace was cozy in the winter, but Meredith much preferred the treelined deck in the summer months.

"Well hello there, Poppy."

Meredith turned, stunned to see Alan Harrison sitting casually at a small table in the bar with a couple of very recognizable A-list actors. As her parents looked at her in shock, Meredith smiled and said a brief hello.

"Your table is ready, Ms. Delaney," the impossibly beautiful and pithy hostess chirped.

"Thank goodness," Meredith said under her breath. She managed to utter the words, "Nice to see you again," as she walked away from the trio of Hollywood royalty.

"Meredith, you have been here for a handful of months, and you're hobnobbing with celebrities?"

"No, Mother. I literally almost knocked him over the other day at a restaurant. His name is Alan Harrison, and he's a screenwriter. I don't really know him, and it's not that big of a deal. Can we change the subject?"

Her parents looked at each other and smiled. "Sure, honey. So, tell us how your book is coming along." Grace Singler carefully repositioned the cloth napkin across her lap, choosing to ignore her daughter's curt tone.

They ended up having a delightful evening, and found it especially charming when the sun went down and the twinkle lights came on. After two hours of gabbing, Poppy was clearly done, so they decided to head home. They put the sleepy tot down for the night and made a pot of coffee to accompany the cherry tart Meredith and her mother had baked earlier that day.

"Meredith, we could not be more proud of you," Dr. Singler said. "We know this has been a painful year for you, and you have definitely risen to the occasion. I'm not going to lie, your mother and I have been worried, but we both feel much more at peace after spending time with you and Poppy over the past few days."

"Thanks, Dad. That means a lot to me."

"I want to hear more about the gala," Meredith's mother said excitedly.

"Well, it's quite an affair," Meredith said with a huge smile. "My adorable next-door neighbor started the foundation, which is why I am even going. She has been so busy lately, but I am sure you will have an opportunity to meet her when things calm down a bit."

Meredith purposely left out the fact that Kathryn's mother was Senator Cahill, and that she had donated one hundred thousand dollars to underwrite the event. Meredith's parents were fiscally conservative and would not have understood parting with that kind of money, even for a good cause.

As the clock chimed midnight, they decided to call it a night, agreeing to reconnect for brunch the following morning.

Chapter 25

Meredith and Poppy greeted Dr. and Mrs. Singler outside Rulli's just before noon. It was a beautiful day, and everyone felt happy and rested. Poppy was in a sundress and matching hat. She had her mother's curls and always received loads of attention wherever she went.

"Hey neighbor!"

Meredith looked up to see Kathryn sitting among a group of local women who congregated for coffee after their daily run.

"Kathryn, I'd like you to meet my parents."

Kathryn jumped up and shook their hands enthusiastically, telling them how much she adored living next door to their daughter and granddaughter.

"Well, she's a sweetheart," Meredith's mother said as they sat down to eat.

"I really hit the jackpot in the neighbor department."

"Is she married?"

"Nope. She works all the time. She dates here and there, but nobody serious."

"Good for her," Grace Singler said. "When it's the right time, she'll know. She seems like she really has her act together."

"Well, I have no intention of getting married again. I met the perfect guy, had the perfect baby, and am perfectly happy living alone."

Out of the corner of her eye, Meredith noticed her parents glance at each other, sharing a look of sadness.

"Meredith, you shouldn't rule anything out. You're still very young, and it hasn't even been a year since Peter's death," Dr. Singler said.

It was still like a knife to the gut when she heard "Peter" and "death" uttered in the same sentence. "I know, Dad."

At that moment, Poppy spilled her juice all over the table, causing all three to simultaneously jump up from their chairs. Meredith ran inside to grab something to mop it up with. As she emerged with a fistful of white terrycloth towels, she found her parents talking to Alan.

She approached the table with a brief smile, nervously flipping the towels from one hand to the other. She could not figure out why she felt so unsettled every time she came into contact with this man, but it was becoming increasingly frustrating.

"Well, hello, Meredith. How funny that we keep running into each other like this."

"Um, yeah," Meredith said, haphazardly mopping up the sticky mess.

"I just ran into Kathryn Cahill, and she mentioned that you are planning to attend the gala."

"I am," Meredith said in a monotone.

"Well, maybe I'll see you there. You'll have to save me a dance."

As he walked away toward his car, Meredith rolled her eyes again.

"Meredith, I think he fancies you," her mother said, lightly slapping her arm.

"Mom, please don't start."

"I'm not! He's just so handsome, Meredith. Plus, look how much you have in common. Both writers. Sounds perfect to me," she said in a singsong voice.

Dr. Singler looked at Poppy and said, as if whispering a secret under her floppy sun hat, "Someday, you will be the one rolling your eyes at your mother."

They all laughed as Poppy shrilled in response to her grandfather's silliness.

"Okay, time to go," Meredith said.

"Meredith, we'd love to spend the day at the beach. What do you think?" her mother said, grabbing her hand.

"Sure, Mom. We could go to Stinson. It won't be too crowded, since it's the middle of the week. We could stop at the deli on the way and have a late lunch on the beach."

"Lovely," Grace Singler said.

The day was perfection. Sunny but not too hot, with the slightest hint of a breeze. They snacked on sandwiches and fruit, with the most decadent chocolate brownies for dessert.

"If I'm going to fit into my dress Saturday night, I'd better keep it to a half of this brownie," Meredith joked.

"Oh, don't be ridiculous. You look fantastic," her mother snapped. Meredith had always been slim, and she took pride in keeping fit with yoga and Pilates. "Do you still drink those kale smoothies?"

"Yep, every morning," and Meredith laughed as her mother visibly shuddered at the thought.

"We'd better go soon," Meredith said. "Our little girl is starting to lose steam."

They collected their blanket and lunch remnants and hiked the short distance back to the car. The drive home took less than thirty minutes, and Poppy thankfully fell fast asleep before they reached the main road.

"So, what time does the benefit begin on Saturday, Meredith?"

"Um, I think cocktails are at six and dinner is served at seven. Then there's dancing and some auction, but I probably won't stay for that."

"Oh yes you will, young lady," her mother said firmly. "Who knows when you will have the opportunity to attend such a fancy affair again? I think you should stay until the bitter end!"

Meredith made eye contact with her father, who was sitting in the passenger seat, and they both chuckled.

"We'll see, Mom."

They all turned in early. The fresh air from the beach was invigorating, but it had proved to be a long day for everyone. The next morning, Meredith took her dress from the full-length hanging bag and steamed it so it would be ready for the following evening.

"Meredith, I don't think I have ever seen a dress this magnificent. You are going to be the belle of the ball, my dear." And with that, her mother gave her a kiss on the cheek and a little tap on the fanny.

Meredith laughed. Her mother was a little overbearing, but she was sweet and always meant well. "Thanks! Hey, I saw this really pretty necklace in Tiburon the other day. I passed on it, but now I'm thinking that it would be perfect with my dress. You will love this store, Mom. Seriously, you walk into Citrus and it just makes you feel good. Want to take a drive with me?"

"Sure, sweetie. I think your dad is tired anyway. He can stay here with Poppy so you and I can have some time together."

"Perfect."

Dr. Singler was happy to have the day to relax in the backyard and catch up on the news while Poppy happily played and napped in the shade.

Meredith and her mother strolled along the main street of Tiburon after deciding that the necklace would indeed be the perfect accessory for her outfit. "Meredith, I know this has been a difficult year for you. Frankly, your dad and I think you have handled it with grace and composure."

"Why do I feel like there is a 'but' coming next," Meredith said, in a tone reminiscent of her teenage years.

"You know me well," her mother laughed. "But. We just don't want you to think that your life is over. After all, you're still in your twenties."

"Mom, who is going to be interested in a widow with a baby?"

"Meredith, open your eyes. Alan Harrison is completely smitten with you!"

Deep down Meredith knew her mom was right. It was driving her absolutely crazy that every time she was near him, he caused her to become unraveled. Even when she met Peter, she didn't initially feel this way. She loved Peter, but this was different. She felt like she could barely breathe when she was in Alan Harrison's presence.

As tears came into Meredith's eyes, her mother hugged her tightly and whispered how much she loved her.

"Fuck the dress," said Meredith. "Let's go next door and get ice cream."

While Meredith's mother didn't typically approve of foul language, she found her daughter's comment funny, and laughed hysterically. "Sounds good, sweetie."

Chapter 26

Meredith allowed herself to sleep in the next morning, which was a rarity and a treat. Her parents had been more than happy to arrive early for Poppy duty, insisting that Meredith be well rested. She knew she should probably write for a few hours, but decided she deserved to take one day off. She was already way ahead of schedule and felt confident that it would make little difference in the end.

She woke up excited about her big night out. She had given some thought to what she and her mother talked about the previous day, and reluctantly considered the concept that she might be able to find happiness with someone else. However, she felt that it was still too soon, and could not totally wrap her head around the idea of being with someone other than Peter.

Meredith spent an hour calming her mind and strengthening her lean body with some of her favorite yoga poses. As always, she ended her practice in Savasana, which gave her a great sense of peace and well-being. As she emerged from her bedroom, she could hear Poppy babbling in the kitchen. The bright-eyed eight-month-old was always happy and, as a result, gave Meredith so much joy.

"Well, hello, Miss Poppy!"

"What time is your massage, Meredith?" her mother asked.

"Oh, I almost forgot." She looked at her watch and was relieved to see she had not missed her appointment.

Meredith walked a few short blocks to a spa that had recently opened. It was a bit extravagant, but she rarely indulged, and she'd heard that the staff was outstanding. After an incredibly relaxing session, she spent twenty minutes in the eucalyptus steam room and left completely primed for the evening's festivities. She stopped at the fruit market and then walked leisurely home, with plenty of time to spare before she needed to get ready for the benefit.

The postman handed Meredith a handful of mail as she approached her house. Mostly catalogs, but on top she noticed an official-looking envelope. She stopped in her tracks when she saw that it was a letter from the FBI.

She entered the house and was relieved to see that her family had not yet returned from their trip to the park. Taking a deep breath, Meredith slowly opened the letter. She noticed immediately that it was signed by Chief Marjorie La Croix. Meredith felt tears stinging her eyes. Her pain was still so close to the surface, and this letter from the FBI immediately brought back horrific memories of the previous year.

The lengthy letter advised Meredith that the investigation into Peter's death had concluded, and it had been determined that she was in no further danger. The envelope also contained a check from the government in the amount of five hundred thousand dollars; the letter advised her that enclosed was a nonnegotiable sum that the government extended in unfortunate and unforeseen situations.

"Unfortunate," Meredith said out loud, shaking her head in disapproval of the FBI's insensitive choice of wording. While the memory of that day brought back sadness, she felt glad to know that she and Poppy were finally safe. She had decided early on not to spend her days worrying, but she still could not break the habit of looking over her shoulder each time she left her house.

When Meredith's parents returned, Grace Singler put down Poppy and went immediately to her daughter. "What is it, Meredith?"

Meredith wiped her eyes and handed her mother the letter. Her father read over his wife's shoulder, and both embraced their daughter. "Five hundred thousand? Well, that seems like a drop in the bucket to me," Dr. Singler spat.

"It's over, Dad. That's all I really care about."

"Sweetie, why don't you lie down for a while," Meredith's mother said, rubbing her back.

Meredith recalled Peter's message of the week before. She was finally beginning to understand his parting words. Feeling a surge of inner strength, she said, "Honestly, I can choose to wallow in despair, or I can move forward and be the example that Poppy deserves. Peter was a great man, and he would not want me to live the rest of my life in fear and sadness."

Smiling through their tears, her parents looked at her with immense respect. She had already come so far, and clearly had turned yet another corner that afternoon.

Chapter 27

D r. and Mrs. Singler gave Meredith some space to digest the events of the day. The house was especially quiet while Poppy napped, which was exactly what Meredith needed. She prepared a cup of tea and scanned the *Marin Independent Journal*. She immediately noticed a sizable write-up of the gala, with a laundry list of the local and national celebrities expected to attend. Naturally, the article made Meredith a little nervous, but also very excited. After all, she absolutely adored her dress and, at the very least, had a feeling it would be a night to remember.

Her parents returned in plenty of time to keep an eye on Poppy while Meredith spent more than her customary twenty minutes primping and dressing for the evening's festivities. As she emerged from her bedroom everyone smiled, including Poppy. There was no doubt that Meredith was going to fit in nicely.

"You look beautiful, Meredith. Now, off you go. Don't worry about anything here. We'll be just fine," Meredith's mother said, flinging a hand in the air as if to convince her daughter that she had total control of the situation.

"I'll have my phone, so if you need anything, call me." And with that, she was off.

Meredith had expected it to be fancy, but she'd had no idea there would be photographers. She immediately saw Kathryn, who waved her over and gave her a huge hug. The flashes blinded Meredith, causing her to nervously giggle. She simply could not get over the fact that she was going to be spending the evening socializing with actors and rock stars.

"Hello, Meredith."

Meredith turned and saw Alan Harrison standing casually for the photographers. He seemed so comfortable in his own skin, she thought.

"Hi, Alan. It's nice to see you again."

He kissed her lightly on the cheek, which immediately sent the photographers into a frenzy, and all Meredith could see was a sea of flashing lights.

"Let's go inside. It's a little crazy out here," Alan whispered.

"I agree. How did you ever get used to this?"

"That's why I live in Marin. The photographers are far less invasive than in Los Angeles. But they do come out of the woodwork for events like this one."

As they entered the room, Meredith was mesmerized by the decor. It was a sea of crisp white linens, with enormous sprays of flowers. Huge crystal chandeliers showered the guests with a glowing soft light. According to Kathryn, a well-known event planner was the mastermind behind the A-list event, and she had, Meredith thought, done a spectacular job.

"Mer, we're at table one," Kathryn said, approaching from across the room.

"What a nice surprise, Meredith," Alan said. "I'm at table one, as well."

Meredith decided to allow herself a slightly new outlook on Alan Harrison. She was by no means seeking anything serious, but she could no longer deny their chemistry.

"Can I get you a cocktail, Meredith?"

"Sure. How about a vodka martini?"

"Good choice. I think I might join you. Be right back."

Meredith soaked in the eclectic collection of guests, all of whom seemed to know one another. She had always been a bit of a wallflower when it came to mingling, and she did not mind standing back to simply observe the cast of characters. She felt as though she were in the middle of a movie as Alan returned with their drinks in hand. With him he brought the governor of California, as well as the head of some tech company in Silicon Valley. They appeared genuinely interested when Meredith told them she was a Stanford alum, and in the midst of writing a fictional series. Alan seemed a bit taken aback, but not shocked, by the brief exchange of pleasantries.

"So, you're a Cardinal? I'm afraid that's going to pose a problem." Alan smiled and took a sip of his martini.

"Oh? Why is that?"

"I went to Cal. Bitter enemies, you know."

"Well, it was nice knowing you," and she turned as if to walk away.

"Not so fast. I think I might be able to move beyond it if you promise me a dance tonight."

"Well, I suppose I could do that," Meredith said with a cute twist of the mouth.

At that moment Kathryn tapped Meredith on the shoulder and said, "Mer, I'd like to introduce you to my parents. Can I steal her away for a minute, Alan?"

"Only for a minute," he said.

As Meredith and Kathryn walked away, Meredith said, "So, how long have you known Alan?"

"We've known each other since college. We lived in the same dorm freshman year. He is a really nice guy, Mer. I know he looks like he could be kind of a player because he is so incredibly handsome, but he's totally not. A few years ago, his wife and son died in a tragic car accident. It was the saddest thing ever, and it nearly destroyed him. They were high school sweethearts, and totally in love. Ever since her death, all the over-Botoxed, over-processed divorcees of Marin have been trying to get their claws into him."

They finally found Kathryn's parents, who were in the center of quite an illustrious group of heavy hitters. Kathryn made the introduction and then began reminiscing with a couple who had known her since she was in nursery school.

Claire Cahill said, "Meredith, Kathryn has told us so much about you and your daughter. The next time we are in Larkspur, we must all have dinner together."

"That would be lovely, Senator Cahill."

"Please, call me Claire. Oh, and this is Kathryn's father, Nathan. Nathan, this is Kathryn's neighbor, Meredith Delaney. She's the gal who moved here from Portland."

"Oh, yes. How nice to meet you, Meredith. I'm sorry, but will you excuse me, dear? Have a nice evening." And with that he was on to a more socially beneficial discussion.

Meredith wondered how the hell Kathryn could have turned out so down-to-earth when her parents seemed so snooty.

Kathryn thanked the group of political dynamos, who had attended only as a favor to her parents, and then grabbed Meredith's hand and whispered, "Let's get the fuck outta here while they're not looking."

"Wow, Kathryn! You could not be more different from your parents," Meredith said, laughing.

"I know. I swear I was switched at birth."

As they approached table one, Alan quickly stood and pulled out the chair next to him for Meredith.

"Thanks, Alan," Meredith said.

"I am not sure if I told you earlier, but you are the most beautiful woman here. I feel fortunate to be the one sitting next to you, Meredith."

She smiled with appreciation, but also with slight embarrassment. She was not accustomed to being the pretty girl at the party, and it threw her for a moment.

As Kathryn looked on from across the table, she smiled to herself. There was no question in her mind that she was looking at two lost souls who had finally found each other.

Chapter 28

Dinner was unbelievable. It was like a who's who of celebrity chefs, and each course was more elaborate than the one before. As dessert and coffee were served, the announcement was made that dancing would continue until ten, and then the auction would promptly commence.

Alan leaned over and said, "The auction gets pretty out of hand. Last year, there was a smackdown between the mayor's wife and this heavy-metal rock star from Mill Valley over a trip to Capri. I've got to give it to her, she might be petite, but she's tougher than she looks!"

Meredith laughed at the thought. Alan was naturally funny, and a terrific conversationalist. She was really enjoying the evening and felt that she and Alan could, at the very least, be very good friends.

"Would you like to dance?" Alan asked. "After all, you did promise."

"I would love to," Meredith smiled.

They danced to nearly every song, and just before the auction began they ducked out to the patio to cool off. The trees twinkled with lights, and the marine air was breezy, but not too chilly.

"Would you be interested in having dinner with me sometime, Meredith?"

"Sure. Baby or sans baby?" she said jokingly.

"Either," he said, and paused. "I don't know if you know this or not, but I lost my wife and son a few years ago. I honestly never thought I'd meet anyone who remotely compared to her. That is, until you almost knocked me over in Sausalito," he said with a wink. "Honestly, I have not been able to get you out of my head since that day."

"Me too. It just took me a little longer to admit it to myself."

Both had tears in their eyes as they removed their fragile coats of armor. Each understood the insurmountable loss the other had experienced, and it was that foundational moment that would ultimately prove to be the catalyst for a second chance at love.

Chapter 29

As the auction began, the anticipation of the high-stakes bidding was mounting. A handful of small but impressive conquests started off the evening: mostly wine, art, and private dinners catered by Bay Area favorites, as well as a lavish brunch for ten at the renowned French Laundry in Napa Valley.

With three items left, the auctioneer took a break so the guests could replenish their beverages and engage in friendly banter about who would take home the coveted grand prizes: another first-class trip to Italy, the use of a beautiful summer house at Stinson Beach, and a walk-on part in a film by Sofia Marquezza, an up-and-coming director who was receiving a great deal of buzz for her soon-to-be-released summer blockbuster.

Meredith excused herself, slipping into the ladies' room to check her lipstick. She also needed to take a moment to contemplate a surprise that she was planning for Kathryn. As she turned the corner, she heard Kathryn say, "Meredith, I've barely had a chance to talk to you all evening. I hope you don't feel like I abandoned you."

"Don't be silly, Kathryn. I am having a terrific time. I have actually spent most of the night getting to know Alan a little better."

"I'm so glad to hear that, Mer," she said, clapping her hands and doing a little impromptu dance.

Meredith laughed, and in a sarcastic tone said, "Excellent dance, Kathryn!"

"Oh, I have to go. The auction is about to resume, and we are close to exceeding last year's total," Kathryn said. She started to make her way through the sea of guests, waving for Meredith to follow.

Meredith returned to the table. As she approached, Alan beamed. He touched her arm lightly as she sat down, placing his hand casually on the back of her chair as they all turned their attention to the auctioneer.

"So, do you plan on raising your paddle for anything else?" Meredith said. Alan had had the winning bid on a case of Gloria Ferrer sparkling wine.

"I don't know. What about you?"

"Maybe," Meredith said with a subtle smile that caused Alan to give her a suspicious grin.

At that point the lights flickered, alerting the guests that the final leg of the auction would soon commence.

The first item up for bid was the walk-on role. There were loads of clamoring wannabe actors who longed for such a privilege. The role went for $150,000. That alone put Kathryn over last year's total by seventy-five thousand. This had truly been a successful event, and Meredith could tell that Kathryn was walking on air.

Next up was the summer house, a four-bedroom beach house overlooking the spectacular Pacific Ocean. Each room had been perfectly appointed with casual chic decor by a local designer who had a waiting list of clients. The starting bid was a steep fifty thousand, and it escalated to ninety thousand in a matter of seconds.

"Wow," Alan said. "This puts last year's auction to shame."

As the fevered bidding reached $175,000, the crowd went crazy. It was as much fun for the spectators as for those engaged in the bidding. During a slight pause, the auctioneer asked for a two-hundred-thousand-dollar bid in hopes of keeping the frenzy going. And quietly but with intention, Meredith raised her paddle and said, "Two hundred thousand."

Alan looked at her in amazement and began cheering wildly, causing the swell of excitement to spill over to the surrounding tables. Before long the room had reached utter chaos. When Kathryn realized who was bidding, she began to cry. Meredith ultimately prevailed, looking forward to a summer at the beach, but also knowing that she was doing the right thing for her friend. Not to mention it was the perfect way to pay tribute to Peter's memory using the monies received from the FBI.

"Any chance I could get an invite to your fancy summer house?" Alan said, as the crowd tried to get a look at the unknown woman who'd swooped in with the winning bid.

"We'll see," she said playfully.

As the crowd began to settle, they were reminded that there was one last item up for bid. It was the trip that had generated so much lively discourse the year before. After the prior exchange, nobody could predict how the bidding would turn out. A nervous hush fell over the grand ballroom. Everyone was still trying to figure out who Meredith was, and why Alan Harrison seemed so infatuated with her.

"We will start the bidding at one hundred thousand dollars."

Several people offered the initial bid, but only three bidders remained serious when the demand reached nearly two hundred thousand. Never before had the prizes commanded such a high offer, and it was turning out to be an evening that the Marin elite would not soon forget.

Meredith sat quietly, thinking that Peter would have loved that her settlement from the FBI was going to such a respectable cause. But more importantly, he would have been proud of the fact that she was happily moving forward with her life.

"Do I hear two hundred fifty thousand?" the auctioneer inquired to the remaining three. One of the bidders raised his paddle, and the other two fell away. It was clearly too rich for their blood, and by the look on the face of the last man standing, he felt certain that he had come away with the winning bid. A bid that would surely keep the locals talking. The auctioneer hollered, "Two hundred seventy-five thousand?"

Again, Meredith quietly raised her paddle. "Two hundred seventy-five thousand."

The room erupted. Alan was laughing hysterically, and Kathryn was so shocked that she stood motionless. Meredith's new nemesis was clearly not happy, and reluctantly raised the offer to $280,000. Though she knew she could only bid up to three hundred thousand, Meredith felt good knowing that she was increasing the amount that the foundation would ultimately receive. She went to $290,000, bluffing that she would go as high as needed.

"Two hundred ninety-five thousand?" the overwhelmed auctioneer said.

Meredith's opponent said, "Two hundred ninety-five thousand."

To which Meredith said, "Three hundred thousand," without missing a beat. It was all she had, and she was going big or going home.

"It's yours," her opponent said. And he stood and comically bowed to her, which caused the room to fill with laughter. People stood on chairs to witness the mayhem that ensued at the front of the grand ballroom. Meredith had secured her place as the queen of the night, though she had no interest in such a title. It was a virtual anomaly for a social nobody to swoop in, spend the evening on the arm of one of the most eligible bachelors in Marin, and then procure the two most coveted prizes.

"Meredith, would you care to share with the class?" Kathryn said, hands on her hips.

Meredith smiled and hugged her friend. "I just wanted to make sure you were well over last year's donations."

"How can I ever repay you, Mer?"

"There is one way," she said in a very serious tone. "Please don't invite me to dinner the next time your parents are in town!"

Both women laughed hysterically as the photographers captured the unprecedented moment, which would likely find its way to the front page of the morning paper.

"You continue to be full of surprises," Alan said to Meredith.

"It must seem that way," she replied, shrugging her shoulders and shaking her head from side to side.

"It's still early. Would you like to join me for a nightcap? I think the bar at the Lark Creek Inn is still open."

"I would love to."

And with that, they walked past the crowd of Bay Area socialites, leaving them wondering what had just happened.

Chapter 30

The bar was nearly empty, with only the flicker of the fireplace to cast a faint glow on the room.

"I'll have a brandy," Meredith said.

"Make that two," Alan said, without taking his eyes off her. "I have to say, Meredith, I am rarely shocked. But tonight I was blown out of the water. I can honestly say that I have never met a woman quite like you: smart, accomplished, assertive. I am also convinced that you have no idea how stunningly beautiful you are."

Meredith blushed as she took a sip of her drink. Alan gently touched her hand as she nervously outlined the rim of her glass with the tip of her finger. The attraction was clear, and Meredith felt an overwhelming sense of exhilaration. They talked for over an hour, eventually realizing that the restaurant had closed in the course of their conversation.

"I think they're trying to tell us something," Alan said, glancing to his right.

As Meredith looked at the remaining two employees, they yawned, looking beyond exhausted. She laughed and nodded in agreement. Alan thanked the staff for their trouble by leaving a very generous gratuity. As he held Meredith's coat for her, she could feel that familiar lurch in her stomach. It had been a long time since she'd had such an enjoyable night. Alan gently took her hand as they walked the few short blocks back to the venue where the auction had taken place, and they promised to meet for dinner the following evening. Meredith felt confident her parents would be happy to watch Poppy. After all, it was at her mother's encouragement that she had decided to pursue a friendship with Alan.

As Meredith pulled her keys from her clutch, they locked eyes for what seemed like an eternity. Alan put his arms around her and pulled her close. She responded immediately, and his hand slid inside her coat, barely touching the back of her evening gown.

They slowly pulled away. While it was premature, Meredith left with the hope that their magical evening would be the first of many.

Chapter 31

Meredith took a moment on the porch before entering the house. The cool air felt good, and she needed to reassess the events of the evening. She knew that her mother would descend upon her right away, wanting every last detail. For the time being, she decided to be discreet. Frankly, she was not sure how much she was willing to share with anyone before she spent more time getting to know Alan.

"Hey, sweetie. How was the gala?"

"Hi, Mom. It was the most beautiful party I have ever attended. The food was fantastic, and it was like a who's who of local celebs. How was Poppy?"

"Perfect! She's the most amazing baby, Meredith," her mother said, switching off the TV.

"Mom, would it be possible for you and Dad to watch Poppy again tomorrow evening?"

"Sure. Big plans?"

"Just dinner. But it could be kind of late."

"We don't mind, sweetie. Anyone special?"

"Actually, it's Alan Harrison," Meredith said, diverting her eyes from her parents while kicking off her heels.

Grace Singler's expression brightened, but she knew if she pushed too hard, her daughter would surely withdraw. Meredith had always been very tight-lipped about her private life, and there was no reason to believe this situation would be any different. They said their goodbyes, immediately revisiting the subject of Meredith's romantic prospect as soon as the car doors closed.

Meredith slept well and woke to the delicious sound of Poppy cooing in her crib.

"Well, hello, girlie girl," she said as she entered the nursery.

Poppy squealed with excitement as Meredith gave the tot a raspberry on her bare tummy.

"Let's get some milk for you, and a great big pot of coffee for your mommy."

Meredith loved the way the morning sun came in through the wall of windows that stretched along the back of the house. She often opened the French doors to welcome the cool morning breeze. At noon, she and Poppy were still in their pajamas. Poppy played happily while Meredith checked her email. She was thrilled to find a response from Spencer, who'd made no changes whatsoever to the additional four chapters that she had sent earlier in the week, although he was anxious to know when she would have more. Meredith figured she would have time to write with more regularity once her parents returned to Portland. For now, Spencer would just have to wait.

Meredith turned her computer off and dressed for the day. She and her parents had reservations to take a tour of the famed Gloria Ferrer wine caves, ending with a private wine and cheese pairing in the picturesque vineyard.

As they arrived home from their afternoon in Sonoma, Meredith received a text from Alan, making sure they were still on for the evening. She replied immediately, telling him that she was looking forward to their date. He suggested that he cook for them and took the liberty of sending her his address. She paused, then sent him a quick "Sounds good," coupled with a wink emoticon.

Standing in front of her closet, she decided that she would go casual since they were staying in for the evening. She wore a pair of white jeans, a blue-and-white-striped boat-neck T-shirt, and a pair of fuchsia flats. She tied it all together with her favorite chunky necklace and a leopard belt, which made her outfit look simple but put-together. At the last minute, she grabbed a blue blazer in case they sat outside. Meredith had always been known for her outstanding fashion sense. It was a perfect combination of colors and patterns, which together made it look as though she had walked out of a magazine.

"You look great, Meredith. What's the plan?" her mother said.

"Alan is cooking."

"Impressive," Meredith's dad said. "If I'd cooked for your mother, she never would have married me."

They all laughed, and Meredith's mother said, "That's for sure."

"Come here, Poppy, and give Mama a smooch."

Poppy, already in her jammies after their big day, was about an hour from going to bed. After a big wet kiss from her daughter, Meredith gave each of her parents a hug and was out the door.

Chapter 32

Meredith turned the corner and was surprised to find herself in front of a formidable Spanish-style house that overlooked Phoenix Lake. She felt like she could reach out and touch Mount Tam, which was what the locals called the grand Mount Tamalpais, a mountain that could easily be seen from almost every town in Marin County.

"Holy crap! He lives in a fucking mansion," Meredith said as she pulled onto the pristine pavers that covered his incredibly long driveway. Knocking on the front door, she briefly regretted stopping by the flower shop. Was it weird to bring a man flowers?

"Whatever," she said under her breath. The door opened, and Alan stepped onto the front porch. He gave Meredith a gentle kiss on the cheek.

"Wow, what did I do to deserve flowers? I assume they're for me."

Laughing, Meredith said, "I figured you had plenty of wine after taking home the whole lot of Gloria Ferrer last night. I couldn't just show up empty-handed. After all, you are cooking."

Pulling a simple but beautiful crystal vase from the cupboard, he placed the flowers on the enormous island. He was clearly enchanted by Meredith, and thought it was adorable that she would show up with a bouquet.

"Wine?"

"Always," she said, smiling in a flirty way.

"You can put your coat and bag anywhere. Make yourself at home, Meredith." He handed her a glass of chardonnay. They clinked glasses, and he took a moment to appreciate how incredibly spectacular she looked standing in his kitchen. A bit embarrassed yet totally enthralled by his gaze, she walked over to the window that overlooked the backyard. The house sat on a perfectly manicured lawn that was completely encased with trees and flowers. The spectacular pool, surrounded by the same brick pavers that capped the driveway, overlooked the magnificent lake below. Truly, one of the most amazing views in the area.

Alan walked up behind her and placed his hand on her back, causing Meredith's knees to almost buckle. The energy in the room was palpable. As Meredith turned, Alan took the glass from her and carefully set it on a nearby table. Placing his hands on either side of her face, he pulled her close. They kissed, first slowly, and then with more intensity.

Neither Alan nor Meredith had dated anyone else since the unexpected deaths of their respective spouses. They shared the fact that both had been madly in love when their lives were shattered, and they found it difficult to grasp the concept that anyone would ever compare. They were equally fearful that falling in love again would mean that it could be taken away in the blink of an eye, and both knew they could not survive another significant loss.

Alan said, "Meredith, I know I told you last night, but I have not been able to get you out of my head for the better part of a month."

She smiled slowly, looking directly into his deep blue eyes. "I know what you mean. Honestly, Alan, I have never had such a visceral reaction to anyone in my entire life."

"Good. I thought it was just me," he said. He pulled her close again and kissed her hard on the mouth. Pulling her shirt from her jeans, he moved his hands softly along her back. Meredith's body was far more curvy and athletic than her clothes let on. She was lean but fit, and it was an incredible turn-on to Alan. He had been in the film industry for years, and never understood why women allowed themselves to become so emaciated.

Meredith did not feel nervous at all. In fact, it was the opposite. She was so turned on by Alan, and could not wait for him to make love to her. He took her by the hand and they made their way to the spectacular master suite, which had ten-foot ceilings that only added to the massive grandeur of the house. They dropped their clothes haphazardly on the settee that ran along the foot of the bed.

"Oh my god, Meredith," Alan said as he kissed her breasts. Meredith was wearing only her skimpy bikini undies. He slid his hand over the top and inside the silky material, tracing with his middle finger a slight figure eight that caused her to moan.

She could feel that Alan was totally aroused, and neither could wait any longer. It was unlike anything either had ever experienced. Before they knew it, almost three hours had passed. They lay in bed watching the sun slowly go down, feeling as if they had known each other forever.

Chapter 33

"Hungry, Meredith?" Alan said, kissing her neck.

"Famished!"

Alan threw the sheets back, revealing his amazing body. Meredith lay under the crisp white linens, thinking how lucky she was to have found him. It occurred to her that losing his wife must have been devastating, but losing a child was unimaginable.

He pulled on a white T-shirt and a pair of worn jeans, which Meredith found incredibly sexy. Kissing her lightly on the lips, he said, "I'm going to finish dinner. Take your time and come down when you're ready. I thought we could eat poolside, and then take a dip if you are up for it."

Meredith threw on the robe that Alan had left for her. She rolled up the sleeves and eventually found her way downstairs.

"So, you do cook! I thought for sure you would be feverishly scooping a gourmet dinner out of Styrofoam containers."

"Are you kidding? I cook all the time. The result of being a latch-key kid, I guess."

She put her arms around him from behind, kissing his back as he picked up two plates that looked like they could have come from some five-star restaurant.

"Let's go outside," he said with a wink.

Meredith grabbed the bottle of wine and the two glasses containing the chardonnay he'd poured when she first arrived.

It was another perfect evening. They ate by candlelight, next to the pool, at an impeccably set table. Meredith finally understood why people put up with the earthquakes and the exorbitant taxes. The weather and the setting made it all worthwhile.

"When did you do all this?" Meredith said, taking a sip of wine.

"While you were upstairs. I thought it would be romantic," he said, with an intentional lift of his left eyebrow.

"Wow, so you continue to woo a girl knowing she is a sure thing? I like that," Meredith said with a devilish grin.

"Meredith, I will never stop wooing you. I am falling in love with you. I knew it the day you ran into me in Sausalito," he said with a slight catch in his voice.

They enjoyed a terrific dinner and sat under the stars polishing off the bottle of wine.

"Want to take a dip?"

"Sure!"

And with that, she dropped her robe and dove in. Alan was right behind her, and they swam in the warm pool for over an hour. When they emerged, they made love again, under the stars on the chaise lounge, finally settling in front of the outside fireplace. It shed the perfect amount of warmth as the chilly night air descended on Marin.

"So, is it still as difficult for you as it is for me to talk about losing a spouse?" Alan said, pulling a blanket over them.

"It is, but I find that it gets a little easier every day. At first it was so traumatic, I could not even utter Peter's name. Now, I try to remember the good memories, mostly for Poppy's sake."

"She is a beautiful child, Meredith. You must feel so grateful to have her."

Meredith smiled at the thought of Poppy and elected not to ask about losing his son. She figured he would bring the subject up when he was ready. The rest of the evening they spent talking about their own childhoods and families. They discussed their common passion for writing, and Meredith wanted to hear all about his newest script, which was set to begin filming in the fall.

They had enjoyed a perfect evening. But it was almost midnight, and Meredith did not want to take advantage of her parents two nights in a row.

"Thank you for dinner, Alan. I loved it," she said, and kissed him.

"You're welcome. Next time we'll include Poppy, and take her for a swim in the pool."

"She will adore it."

They said goodbye and Meredith left, feeling happier and more at peace than she had in a very long time.

Chapter 34

As Meredith entered the house, she was smiling from ear to ear. Her parents did not press her for details, but they were clearly thrilled for their daughter, who was beginning to open her heart to the possibility that she could find happiness again.

"Did Poppy fall asleep quickly?"

"She was so tired, we barely got through one book," her mother said as she tidied up the toys in the family room.

"Mom, let me do that. You and Dad have done enough."

"You know I don't mind," her mother said, smiling.

"So, I forgot to mention that I had the winning bid on a beautiful beach house at the auction last night. What do you think about spending an extended vacation at Stinson Beach this summer? A little fun, totally relaxing, and more than enough room for all of us," Meredith said, casually fetching some lemonade from the fridge.

"Funny you should bring that up, sweetie, because we already knew," her mother said in a very self-satisfied tone.

"What do you mean, Mom?"

Grace Singler flipped the *Marin Independent Journal* around. On the front page was a photo of Meredith and Kathryn. Both looking exquisite. The headline read, "Who's Marin's Newest Celebrity?"

In slow motion and visibly mortified, Meredith reached for the paper. She sat down while reading the article, which chronicled the entire evening.

"Seriously, Meredith? You gave the entire five-hundred-thousand-dollar settlement to dogs?" her dad said, with an incredibly unsupportive look.

"Okay, I know it seems a little ostentatious, but keeping that money from the FBI did not sit well with me. I want it to go to a charity that is making positive impact, and Kathryn is doing just that. Anyway, I know Peter would have approved," she said curtly.

"Well, sweetie, it's your decision, and we are proud of you nonetheless. Besides, the photo is absolutely beautiful. Can I take this home and show my friends at yoga?" her mother said, revisiting page one of the paper.

While Grace Singler gave the illusion of approving her daughter's decision, her father shook his head, muttering under his breath something about the cost of college, and the hope that in his next life he would come back as a dog from Marin County.

"Uh, sure, Mom," Meredith said, still embarrassed by the thought of being on every coffee table in Marin.

Meredith's parents could tell she no longer wanted to discuss the matter. Ever since she was a child, she had a way of making her feelings abundantly clear, and this was no exception. In an effort to change the subject, Meredith suggested that, since her parents only had two more days before going home, they venture into the city and stay overnight.

"Well, that sounds like fun," Dr. and Mrs. Singler said in unison.

"All right, then I will make a reservation, and we'll go first thing in the morning. By the way, thanks again for the last two nights. I really appreciate your taking care of Poppy for me."

Embracing her daughter, Grace whispered that she was so proud of her, and would do anything to see her happy. Both had tears in their eyes as they pulled away.

Meredith saw them off. "Drive safely," she said. She was sad to think that they were leaving and made a mental note to ask them again about returning for the summer.

Meredith heard the familiar chime indicating a new text had arrived. Reaching for her phone, she smiled when she realized it was from Alan. All it said was, "xo."

Chapter 35

he next day Meredith packed the car and arrived at her parents' hotel early. They were all very excited about spending the next few days shopping and indulging at their favorite eateries. The weather was unseasonably warm, which always made it more fun.

After checking in at the Four Seasons they took in the spectacular view from their suite, then unpacked while discussing lunch options. Meredith dug for her cell phone, which was ringing from the depths of Poppy's diaper bag.

"Hello?" she said, not knowing if she'd caught it before it went to voice mail.

"When can I see the most beautiful woman in Marin again?"

Recognizing Alan's deep voice, she said, smiling, "I'm in the city with my parents."

"I'm actually going to be coming in this afternoon. Maybe we can all have dinner together?"

"I think that could be arranged," she said.

Her mother gave her a curious look.

"I'll make reservations at Gary Danko," Alan said.

"First of all, we have a baby, and second, there is no way we are going to get in with such short notice. You have to call at least two weeks in advance."

"Leave it to me. I'll meet you there at seven o'clock. I am looking forward to meeting your parents, Meredith."

"Oh, man, this is either going to be really good or really bad," Meredith said under her breath as she hung up.

"Ready, sweetie?"

"Yep, I'm starving, and Poppy is going to get cranky if she doesn't eat soon, too."

They had a beautiful lunch at one of Dr. Singler's favorite restaurants, and afterward shopped while Poppy took a long nap in her stroller. Meredith was relieved that she would be well rested for the evening, but she was becoming increasingly worried about dinner. She could not believe she was taking a baby to such a swanky restaurant.

"Well, honey, look at it this way: if Poppy doesn't cooperate, we'll come back to the hotel and order in. It will give us something to tease her about when she's a teenager!"

Grace Singler always had such a great outlook on every situation. For as long as Meredith could remember, her mother's motto had been, "Don't sweat the small stuff, it's just not worth it!"

They returned to the hotel with plenty of time to relax and dress for dinner. Both Meredith and her mother had purchased new outfits, since they would be dining at a fancier restaurant than previously expected. Dr. Singler almost always wore a blazer, so he was perfectly fine, although he did put on a fantastic tie that Meredith's mom had found at Saks.

Right on time, they walked into the best restaurant in San Francisco. The host greeted them warmly and took their coats right away.

"If you'll follow me, please."

"And so it begins," Meredith whispered to her mother.

They were ushered across the dining room. In one corner the Speaker of the House of Representatives was engaged in an intimate dinner with friends, and in the other was some actor that Meredith recognized but could not place, wining and dining what looked like a supermodel. Oddly enough, the staff did not seem at all surprised that Meredith was carrying a baby on her hip as they made their way through the posh digs.

"Welcome," Alan said as the host delivered them to a beautifully decorated private dining room. He kissed Meredith on the cheek and shook hands with Dr. and Mrs. Singler.

"I am so relieved that we are not in the main dining room," Meredith said. "You must have pulled some serious strings to get this room."

Though he remained unaffected by the connection, Alan said, "The owner is an old friend. So, can I interest anyone in a cocktail?"

Once the drinks and appetizers arrived the group settled in nicely, primarily discussing the gala. Alan explained in detail how much of a superstar their daughter had been that night.

"That is not true," Meredith said, laughing.

"Don't listen to her. She was calm, cool, and collected; she created quite a frenzy. It probably still has the social circles buzzing."

"Well, it's a good thing I don't spend any time in the social circles," Meredith said, rolling her eyes.

Dinner flew by and everyone clearly enjoyed the food and the company. Poppy was thrilled that she could play quietly with her toys and not be confined to a high chair. As the successful evening came to an end, they exited into the marine breeze. Alan put his hand on Meredith's back as they walked to the car. She desperately wanted to kiss him but felt uneasy with her parents lingering behind.

Meredith's mother said, "Tell you what, why don't we take Poppy to the hotel, and you two can go out for a drink or something."

"Are you sure, Mom?"

"Absolutely!"

And with that, they said their goodbyes, and Meredith and Alan walked down the street hand in hand.

Chapter 36

They reached the marina and perched on a bench, appreciating the unseasonably warm night air.

"I've wanted to kiss you all night, Meredith," Alan said in her ear.

Extremely turned on, she said, "Well, I suggest you do something about that."

Alan pulled her close, kissing her neck with increasing passion, wishing they could spend the night together, but knowing it would be impossible.

"I could tell my parents really liked you, Alan. Believe me, if my dad didn't approve of you, everyone at the table would have known," she said with a giggle.

"That's good to know." He slid his hand into her coat, caressing her breast.

"Alan, you really shouldn't start something you can't finish," Meredith said with a raised eyebrow.

"So, when do these lovely people plan on leaving town?" he said, in a way that made Meredith laugh hysterically.

"Day after tomorrow."

With a deep sigh, he said, "I guess I can wait."

Meredith slipped into the hotel after her teenage make-out session, feeling a little naughty. She quickly checked on Poppy, who was out, and not moving a muscle. Dr. and Mrs. Singler had long since fallen asleep, and Meredith figured she should do the same. After all, they had another big day ahead of them before her parents returned to Portland.

Chapter 37

They woke up to a traditionally foggy San Francisco morning, but still enjoyed the day. They took their customary lap around the famed Museum of Modern Art, taking in the exhibit of photographs by Garry Winogrand, one of the more important and well-respected photographers of the twentieth century. Afterward, they lollygagged at the museum's Blue Bottle Coffee Bar, each indulging in a cappuccino and a piece of the highly sought-after Mondrian Cake.

"Meredith, we have had such a wonderful vacation," her mom said, as they relaxed with a second cup of coffee.

"Me, too," she said. "Say, have you given any more thought to Stinson Beach this summer?"

"As a matter of fact, we have," her dad said. "We would love to spend a few weeks with you and Poppy this summer. We will be in Paris in June, but July is wide open. I've racked up so many vacation days, I could probably retire today." He laughed at his own joke.

"That's great," Meredith said, picking up Poppy's crumbly mess from the floor.

They reluctantly made their way back to Marin, where thankfully the sun was shining. Meredith could not get over the Bay Area weather. It seemed like every mile north of the Golden Gate Bridge added one more degree to her car's temperature gauge.

They sat in the backyard, reading and chatting happily while Poppy napped. Meredith heard the familiar laugh of her friend from over the fence.

"Hey, Kathryn, if you're not doing anything tonight, want to join us for a glass of wine?"

"Love to, Mer! I am heading out for a run, but how about six or so?"

"Perfect! See you in a bit."

The evening's impromptu gathering turned into a small party. A few other neighbors were out, so Meredith decided the more the merrier. She even called Alan, who was thrilled by the invitation.

"Meredith, I had no idea you were an artist," Alan said. He stood in front of the fireplace, admiring the illustrious martini painting. "What can I do to persuade you to paint something for me?"

"I'll let you know," she said in a soft, throaty voice.

Everyone had a great time. By midnight, Meredith's parents thought it best to get back and pack, as their flight left at noon the following day.

"Can I help you clean up, Meredith?" Alan offered after the rest of the guests had gone home.

"Not until you come over here and give me a proper kiss," she said.

When they were together, it was as if they had known each other for a lifetime. There was something about their energy that made Meredith certain they were meant to be together. She no longer felt like moving on meant that she was, in any way, diminishing the life that she once shared with Peter. She understood now what Peter had meant when, in her recent reverie, he'd implored her to follow her instincts, trusting that it was time to move forward.

"I am completely in love with you, Meredith," he said as he passionately kissed her.

"I know it seems so quick, but I feel the same way. I honestly never thought I would ever find love again."

And with that, Meredith took him by the hand, ignoring the mess in the kitchen, and led him straight to her bedroom.

Chapter 38

The following morning Alan left before Poppy woke. He knew that Meredith planned to meet her parents for breakfast before their flight departed, and figured they would prefer to spend their last few hours as a family.

Meredith felt a bit sad after seeing them off, although the fact that she had a significant amount of writing to submit forced her to keep her mind clear and focused. Poppy was absolutely exhausted after their busy week, and she took a three-hour nap that afternoon. Meredith took advantage of the quiet and slammed out two more chapters. She basically followed her initial outline, but also took the liberty to deviate when she felt inspired to do so.

Kathryn tapped on the front door. Without missing a beat, she said, "Tell me everything!"

"I'm surprised it took you this long to knock on my door," Meredith said, shaking her head.

"Let me start by saying that you and Alan are perfection as a couple. Now, tell all!"

"Honestly, Kathryn, I never really believed in love at first sight, but that's exactly what happened. It took me a little longer to finally admit it to myself, but I just couldn't deny it once we spent time getting to know each other. Wine or coffee?"

"Um, hello, wine," said Kathryn in a sarcastic but very funny tone.

"Red or white?"

"Whatever! Just give me the gory details, Mer!"

"Okay. We had a great time at the gala and went out for drinks at Lark Creek afterward. From there, yada yada yada, and we're basically a couple."

"You can't yada yada me, Mer!"

"All I can say is that it is as if we have known each other forever, and I am fairly certain I am falling in love with him."

"Oh, Mer," Kathryn said smiling.

At that point, Poppy started squealing happily from her crib. Meredith had not given any thought to dinner, but she now noticed that the afternoon had somehow flown by.

"Care to join us for supper, Kathryn? I could make salmon."

"I love having a gourmet neighbor who is also rich and generous," Kathryn said, laughing. "I have a dozen cupcakes from SusieCakes that I bought this morning in a moment of weakness. I'll run over and get them."

"What's SusieCakes?"

"Only the best bakery in Marin. Be right back."

Meredith laughed at her friend and said to Poppy, "Kathryn is so silly," as she pulled a few dinner items out of the fridge.

The phone rang while she was marinating the salmon. "Hello?" said Meredith.

The line went dead.

"That's weird. Probably a wrong number," she said out loud.

"Okay, I'm back, Mer. Aren't these cupcakes the most beautiful works of art? And they are delicious, too!"

Meredith prepared the perfect dinner while Kathryn played with Poppy on the floor.

"Let's eat on the patio. Sound good?"

"Sounds great," Kathryn said.

They enjoyed a great dinner, followed by the delectable confections Kathryn contributed, then moved inside as the evening grew chilly. Meredith eventually put Poppy to bed as Kathryn cleaned up the kitchen.

"Well, aren't you a sweetheart, Kathryn. You didn't have to clean up all by yourself."

"Please, it's the least I could do."

"Did I hear the phone ring?"

"Yeah, but when I answered it the line was dead. Probably a wrong number."

Meredith had a moment of panic, but convinced herself that it was nothing. After all, the FBI had concluded its investigation and determined that the al-Qaeda connection posed no further danger. Still, she could not help but feel a slight bit of trepidation at the thought of two strange calls back to back.

Putting the incident aside, she and Kathryn settled in and watched *Something's Gotta Give*, with Diane Keaton and Jack Nicholson. Both had the film at the top of their all-time-favorite list and never grew tired of it.

"Thanks for a great evening, Mer. I am so happy for you and Alan," said Kathryn.

"Good night, Kathryn."

Kathryn waltzed down the front steps and over to her house. Meredith locked up, feeling for the first time a little uneasy. She managed to talk herself out of being scared by telling herself it was nothing.

Chapter 39

Meredith and Poppy spent the next day cleaning the house and replenishing the pantry. Meredith made a concerted effort to move beyond her scare from the night before and decided to chalk it up to a fluke. Alan invited them over for dinner and a swim, and Meredith gladly accepted.

"Okay, little miss, you need to take a nap. We have a big evening ahead of us."

Meredith completed another chapter and sent it off to Spencer, feeling like the manuscript was coming together nicely.

That evening was a success. They barbecued and swam until Poppy was exhausted. She loved the water, and it made Meredith's heart swell when she saw how sweet Alan was with her. Meredith often thought how difficult it must be to be around children after enduring such a painful loss. But Alan was never anything but kind and generous to both of them.

"I need to put this little one down," Meredith said.

"Oh! I almost forgot. Check this out, Meredith."

He took her by the hand and led her to a small room next to the master. It contained a white crib with the sweetest pink gingham bedding. There was even a matching pink chair in the corner.

"I can't believe you did all this, Alan."

"Why? We can't have Poppy sleeping on a subpar travel bed when she is here." He appeared totally incensed at the thought.

Laughing, Meredith said, "Thank you, Alan."

"Would you like to stay here tonight? After all, Poppy should really give her new bed a whirl," he said in a very serious tone, coupled with a devilish grin.

"A convincing offer, I must say."

"It's settled, then."

They put the baby to bed. She was happily snoozing the second the lights dimmed. Still in their swimsuits, they took the baby monitor outside and shared the oversize chaise, admiring a full moon that lit up the entire sky. It was not long before Alan pulled Meredith onto his lap, and they quickly discarded their suits. He started kissing her neck, moving down to her breasts, and then lower. Exhilarated, they made love under the stars, then retired to the house for the duration of the evening.

"Meredith, I don't think I will ever get enough of you."

They made their way to the master suite after Meredith looked in on Poppy. She was happily sleeping in her pretty room, which warmed Meredith's heart.

"How's Poppy?"

"Perfect," Meredith said, sliding into bed, while simultaneously taking the initiative. She straddled him, causing him to be pleasantly surprised. He responded immediately and became aroused as she used her tongue to drive him crazy. They eventually moved as one, then fell asleep, waking the next morning still in each other's arms.

Chapter 40

Meredith and Poppy returned home after breakfast the next day. As Meredith puttered around her kitchen, she noticed that the French door was ajar. She stopped in her tracks, paralyzed in the same way that she had been almost two years before, when she arrived home to find the door to the Portland loft open. She surveyed the house and found nothing missing, then called Kathryn to find out if she had seen anything unusual the night before.

"As a matter a fact, Mer, the neighbor's dog was barking more than usual last night. Maybe you should call the police."

"Maybe. I just can't deal with this again, Kathryn." And she began to cry.

Kathryn, becoming increasingly concerned, suggested she call Alan.

"Let's just start by calling the police. Maybe it has nothing to do with me. For all I know it could be a bunch of teenagers just messing around."

A Larkspur officer was at her front door in less than ten minutes. He confirmed that two separate neighbors had seen an unusual woman in the neighborhood, and nobody could identify her. She'd seemed to be walking around looking in windows. By the time the police arrived, she was gone, and there did not appear to be any resulting damage.

"Officer, did they have any description of the woman at all?" Meredith inquired.

"Nothing specific. Just that she was in her mid-twenties and had long blond hair. Feel free to call, Ms. Delaney, if you see anything out of the ordinary or need any further assistance."

"Thank you, Officer."

"Mer, I think you and Poppy should stay with me or at Alan's house tonight."

"Don't be silly, Kathryn. I refuse to look over my shoulder every time some innocuous little thing happens in my general vicinity. After all, I could have easily left the door open when I left yesterday. It's probably just a big coincidence."

"Regardless, call me day or night if you change your mind."

"Thanks, Kathryn."

Meredith put Poppy to bed and cleaned up the kitchen. She decided to take a bath and go to bed early. Feeling much better after soaking for over an hour, she wrapped herself in a robe and made the rounds, turning off lights and double-checking doors. Spotting an envelope out of the corner of her eye, she did a double take. As she got closer, she found the same French door open a crack, and a large manila envelope sitting on the table. All she could see was her first name, written in what looked like red marker.

"Oh my god," Meredith said under her breath. Instinctually, she ran immediately to Poppy's room, only to find an empty crib.

The command leapt off the page through the tears streaming down Meredith's face. The letter was made up of words torn from a magazine, like she had seen so many times in thrillers. Barely unable to read through her hysteria, she was finally able to focus enough to decipher the text. It simply said, "I know you received $500,000. If you want your little flower back, you will do as I say. No police. No phone calls. I am watching you."

Meredith fell to the ground, gasping and sobbing uncontrollably. She did not know what to do, and was flooded with the possibilities that every parent is terrified to consider. Was the person really watching her? Were her phone calls being traced? She could not take any chances.

It was at that moment that her phone rang. She lunged frantically, almost dropping the receiver. Before she could say anything, the person on the other end said, "Cute kid, but if you want her back, you'd better listen carefully."

"Anything. Please don't hurt her. She's all I have in this world."

"Good, then we understand each other. Bring the money to the Marin Headlands in your fancy Louis Vuitton backpack. I will be at the very top, where the road ends. If I even get an inkling that you involved the police, I will throw your little girl off the Golden Gate Bridge."

"Oh my god, please, please don't hurt her."

"Five hundred thousand dollars in hundreds at the Headlands tomorrow at noon."

Meredith stood paralyzed as the line went dead. She ran to the bathroom, violently ill at the thought of losing her baby. How could she possibly survive another loss? On the bathroom floor, she curled up in an impalpable haze. Hours went by and still Meredith remained on the cold tile, unable to assimilate how to best respond to the financial demand in order to bring Poppy home.

As the sun rose, Meredith heard a noise. She emerged gingerly just as Alan walked through the door that remained open from the night before. The air in the house was frigid, but Meredith felt nothing. Barely able to stand, she still gripped the note left by the kidnapper.

"Meredith, what happened? I ran into Kathryn this morning, and she mentioned that you had to call the police last night because of a possible intruder. I knocked on the front door. When you didn't respond, I got worried and came around back."

She remained immobile. He scooped her up, wrapping her shivering body in a blanket. She made a failed attempt to explain what had happened, but said enough that Alan knew the authorities needed to be notified as soon as possible.

"Why didn't you call me?"

Completely dazed, she told him they were watching her and would throw Poppy off the bridge if she told anyone.

"Oh my god, Meredith. We have no choice in the matter. We have to call the police."

She handed him the dysfunctional letter, and again dissolved into tears.

The FBI was immediately apprised of the situation, and within a few hours, a plan had been devised to extract the baby from the hands of the nefarious stranger who had plucked the tot from her crib.

Chapter 41

Chaos descended upon Meredith's small bungalow. Alan canceled his schedule, remaining tethered to her side.

Special Agent Fielding said, "Ms. Delaney, I need to know exactly what she said on the phone. Any small detail could be helpful in locating Poppy."

Meredith tried to recall specifics, but she was finding it almost impossible to concentrate. The last twelve hours had been a blur, causing her to question how much she would be able to contribute to the investigation.

"Okay, let me ask you some questions that may help to trigger your memory."

"Okay," Meredith said in a very frail voice.

"Did her voice have any distinguishing elements?"

"Um, she sounded young, but definitely commanded the conversation. Actually, there was a moment when she spoke that I thought I had heard her voice before."

"Well, let's pursue that, Meredith. What, in her voice, caused you to think that? Was it her tone, the words she chose, her cadence?"

"I don't know. It was familiar, but I just can't place her," Meredith said, racking her brain.

"Okay, let's move on. We'll come back to that later. Did she give you any specific demands, other than the amount of money?"

Meredith's eyes flashed and everyone in the room took notice. She jumped up from the chair and began pacing the room, tapping her finger against her head as if it would somehow clarify her memory.

"My backpack."

"What do you mean?" Alan said.

"She told me to transport the money in my Louis Vuitton backpack."

"Why is that strange, Meredith?" Agent Fielding said.

"Because I gave that bag away before we moved here," Meredith said, visibly experiencing a breakthrough moment.

The agents immediately left a message for Chief Marjorie La Croix at the Portland FBI, who had been placed on notice earlier in the day. They had not made any connections, but now they were convinced it had something to do with the major FBI debacle that nearly cost Marjorie La Croix her job.

As the clock ticked rapidly toward noon, they received a call from Chief La Croix. It turned out that one of their lower-level employees had not shown up for work for two days and could not be located. Chief La Croix had no idea if it was related but thought it noteworthy enough to report.

Agent Fielding generated a profile of the missing employee. Meredith took one look at the photo as it flashed onto the computer screen and nearly collapsed.

"What is it, Meredith?" Alan said.

"It's her. Oh my god, yes. I remember now. She's the receptionist who practically made us beg for her assistance every time we entered the lobby at the FBI headquarters in Portland. She had this way of curling her vowels. Agent Fielding, that is definitely the woman on the phone."

Without missing a beat, they went into action. They had very little time to perfect the master plan and get to the highest peak of Marin, which was known for giving locals and visitors a most impressive view of San Francisco.

With full knowledge of the woman they were dealing with, they felt more certain that they could bring the matter to a safe resolution. But they also knew that until the baby was safe in the arms of her mother, their task was not complete.

Chapter 42

As quickly as the FBI had arrived at the bungalow, they were gone. Meredith and Alan stayed behind for two hours, while the destination was surveyed by the team and a recovery blueprint put into place.

"What if she throws her over the bridge like she said on the phone, Alan? How could I ever move forward?" Meredith said, without any inflection in her voice.

"Listen to me, there is no reason to believe that she will do that. She is obviously after the money, and without Poppy she has no bargaining chip."

As she sat staring at nothing, it suddenly occurred to her that her nightmare must induce painful memories for Alan. After all, it had only been three years since he lost his wife and son on the same day. Looking at Alan as he poured her a cup of tea, she said, "I am so sorry if this is, in any way, causing you to recall the painful memory of Courtney and Matthew."

"Meredith, that was a traumatic period for me, and honestly, you never fully recover. But I am thinking only about you and Poppy right now, and I want nothing more than to be here for you."

"I don't know what I would do without you, Alan," she said through her tears.

Just then the phone rang, notifying them that an agent would pick them up in thirty minutes to take them to the Headlands.

"Oh my god, Alan. I can't believe this is really happening. I am afraid that she will know the FBI agent isn't me and get spooked. What if she panics and does something totally insane?"

"Meredith, I understand that you have little faith in the FBI after your horrific experience, but they are trained to handle these types of situations. We have to trust that they know what they are doing. Let's just think positively, and focus on rocking sweet Poppy to sleep tonight."

Chapter 43

The FBI and local SWAT teams were dispatched to the scene in two unmarked vehicles to ensure that suspicions would not be raised. They established that Diana Collins, who worked for the Portland Bureau, was definitely involved, but it was unclear whether she was acting alone. A female FBI agent, who resembled Meredith in height and hair color, drove Meredith's vehicle, posing as the distraught mother. Another vehicle containing Alan and Meredith remained a safe distance away, so that Collins would not suspect the authorities were closing in on her and make a hasty decision.

With twenty minutes to spare, the team was in place, posing as sightseers casually admiring the view. There was no sign of anyone with a baby or matching the description of Diana Collins. Meredith gazed out the window from the backseat of the generic sedan, not knowing how she had arrived back at this familiar place of grief but entirely certain that she could not survive the loss of her baby girl.

Alan had a firm understanding of the gut-wrenching wave of emotion Meredith was being forced to endure, and he looked into her vacant stare with empathy and compassion. Regardless of the outcome, he knew she would need his strength to navigate to a place where she could feel safe and secure again.

"We have eyes on her," said a voice on the handheld radio.

Meredith initially winced, and she looked blankly into Alan's face.

Their vehicle sat a fair distance away from the scene, and they only knew what they could hear via the airwaves. The powers that be had decided that they could not risk a volatile mother foiling the FBI's plan.

"It's been too long," Meredith said.

"It's only been a few minutes, Meredith. We have to let the FBI do their job, and trust they will bring Poppy back to you," Alan said, taking her into his arms.

The undercover team milled casually around the top perch of the Headlands and subtly observed the black rental car roll to a slow stop. There appeared to be one woman in the vehicle, and it was unclear whether the baby was with her. The agent posing as Meredith pulled her SUV into view. She wore sunglasses and a hat in an effort to convince Diana Collins that she was Meredith, following her instructions to arrive alone and without the authorities.

As the women slowly exited their respective vehicles, the tension was palpable. The agent elected to restrain herself, waiting for Diana to speak first. She grabbed the newly purchased Louis Vuitton bag from the passenger seat, full of marked bills in case the exchange was unavoidable.

Diana Collins was quite obviously a novice. She was visibly shaking and looked as if she had no real plan.

"Throw the bag over here," she said, looking from side to side.

"Not until I have Poppy," the agent said, pretending to cry through her words.

The team of agents knew they had to take Collins down before she pulled the baby from the vehicle. Upon command they rushed the vehicle, and Diana looked up to see that she was surrounded, with no way out. She nervously backed up, moving closer and closer to the seven-hundred-foot, razor-sharp drop. Sobbing uncontrollably, she looked over her shoulder, then back to the sea of firearms that would either kill her or compel her into custody.

"Down on the ground," the agent posing as Meredith demanded, drawing her gun.

Diana Collins looked from one agent to another, saying over and over again, "I am so sorry. I am just so sorry."

"On the ground, Diana."

And with that, she took an intentional step back and, spread-eagle, careened through the shroud of eucalyptus trees to the valley below.

The agent in charge immediately ran to the car and gave the thumbs-up. "We have the baby, and she appears to be just fine," he calmly announced into his earpiece.

Meredith nearly collapsed as she made her way to the scene. As she carefully hoisted the sleeping baby from the car, she could feel Peter's presence around them. She knew in her heart that he'd had a hand in the favorable outcome.

Chapter 44

Little was said as Alan and Meredith drove north to Larkspur, with Poppy babbling happily in the backseat as if nothing significant had occurred. They looked at each other, unable to repress subtle smiles, still struggling to comprehend the events of the day.

The authorities had remained at the scene, pulling the lifeless body from the thick brush. No further participation would be required of Meredith. Between Portland and San Francisco, the FBI had determined that Diana Collins acted alone, having suffered from emotional challenges much of her life. After searching her apartment, the Portland Bureau discovered that she had left behind a diary chronicling her involvement in the al-Qaeda case. From the beginning, Agent Murino had preyed on Diana's instability to get her to assist him with innocuous tasks that would have otherwise caused his superiors to be suspicious of his involvement. The daily entries repeatedly spoke of the millions they would stand to gain when the case was over. When Murino was prematurely killed, Diana blamed Meredith and Peter for destroying her own promise of riches. Learning recently that Meredith had been given the hefty sum as a settlement for Peter's death, she'd seen it as an opportunity to recoup Agent Murino's financial guarantee.

That afternoon, Meredith felt it best to take Poppy to the pediatrician, to make certain the child had not sustained any injuries in the twelve hours she was out of her mother's care. Relieved after the doctor's examination, they arrived home to the sunny bungalow that had always given them so much joy. Alan preemptively arranged for the locks to be changed, which gave Meredith peace of mind.

"Oh my gosh, Meredith, I was so worried," Kathryn said, dashing across the lawn. "What can I do?"

Exhausted and feeling years older than she had the previous day, Meredith hugged Kathryn, telling her that she was just thankful to be home.

"I just put a lasagna in the oven. It will be ready in an hour."

"Thanks, Kathryn. I really appreciate it."

Alan and Meredith put Poppy to bed early, after eating very little dinner. Everyone needed a good night's sleep.

"I have cleared my schedule for as long as you need me, Meredith."

"Alan, I know for a fact you have meetings in Los Angeles later this week to discuss the film. I don't want you to feel like you have to babysit me when you clearly have pressing matters to attend to."

"Sweetie, let me worry about that."

Alan spent the night with Meredith, giving her the emotional support that she needed after the stress of the last few days. He put her to bed, and she fell asleep as soon as her head hit the pillow. He canceled his meetings for the following week. Electing not to go into specifics, he simply said that a personal family issue would require his full attention. Due to the fact that the film was not scheduled to shoot until fall, the director agreed to postpone the pre-filming discussions so Alan could attend to his personal commitments.

The days following the kidnapping were stressful. Fascination with the al-Qaeda connection resulted in the printing of story after story in an effort to keep the salacious details in the news. Meredith declined to comment, as she thought it would only add to the ongoing drama. Thankfully, with little fuel, the matter was soon replaced by unrelated stories, finally allowing Meredith's personal life to become old news.

By the end of May, things finally returned to normal, and Meredith managed to gain momentum on her book. She was happily writing every day and had only a few chapters to complete before finishing the first of three novels. It was a series of thrillers, and Spencer could not be happier with her masterful ability to weave a complex story. He was hopeful that it would become a best seller, propelling both of them to national acclaim. Meredith, on the other hand, felt pride in completing a personal goal. As long as she could remember, being a well-respected author was always one of her greatest dreams. Wealth and notoriety never appealed to her, and frankly, she wanted to remain less in the public eye than she had as of late.

"My goal is to complete book number one by the time we take possession of the house in Stinson Beach for the summer," she said to Alan, nuzzling his ear.

"So, when do I get to read this mysterious manuscript?" he said.

"You can read it now if you want."

"What I want right now is you." And with that, he pulled her on top of him. Meredith knew what made Alan crazy. She began with his neck and slowly moved south, loving the way she made him feel as he became more aroused. He always reciprocated, giving Meredith immense pleasure. Neither tired of finding new ways to make love, and they felt more and more connected every day.

As they lay in bed appreciating the quiet of the night, Alan whispered, "I always want to be with you, Meredith. I also would love the privilege of being able to give Poppy a father as she grows up. Meredith, will you marry me?"

Meredith had tears in her eyes. She felt exactly the same, and happily accepted his proposal to be a husband, as well as a father to her beloved Poppy.

Chapter 45

"So, anyone interested in ring shopping today?" Alan pulled Meredith close, kissing her until she opened her eyes.

Smiling, Meredith said, "I have bad news for you."

"Oh, really. Change your mind already?"

"I am sorry to say that you've hooked up with a girl who doesn't really like fancy diamond rings. And while we're at it, I have no intention of having plastic surgery or sticking needles in my face to erase every little wrinkle," she said, giggling, yet in an infinitely serious tone.

"Good! I've never understood why people fall into that unpleasant habit. Sad, really. You know what makes people feel youthful, Meredith?" he said, tugging at her silky boy shorts.

"What's that?" she said, softly moaning.

"Come here and I'll show you."

After a lovely early-morning romp, they enjoyed coffee on the patio until Poppy woke up. All three were getting along famously, experiencing a well-deserved happiness after facing too much pain and loss.

"I think it's time that you and Poppy move in with me, Meredith."

"But I love this place. I love the way the sun comes in the windows, and the way the floors creak."

"Is that your way of telling me you don't like my house?"

"No, no, no! It's just a bit grand and fancy. Plus, we couldn't walk to Rulli's or Lark Creek for dinner, and . . ."

"Okay, I get it. You want to stay close to town. Simple solution; I'll sell my house and we'll buy whatever you want here in Larkspur."

"Seriously?"

"Anything you want."

"Are you sure you could give up your beautiful estate, Alan?"

"Sweetie, it's just a thing. Things mean nothing to me. I want you and Poppy to be happy, and I can live anywhere, as long as it's with you."

She loved that he felt as she did about stuff. Meredith could be happy in the bungalow, but she knew in her heart it was much too small for three, as she made her way into the kitchen from the backyard.

Meredith chirped from the kitchen, "I want the bungalow, but just a smidge bigger."

"What if we have a whole slew of babies," Alan said, sneaking up behind her and swatting her fanny.

"Ooh, I would love that. I can live with a basketball team, but no bigger," she joked.

"Including us, or excluding?"

"Including! Are you crazy?"

"You know, Meredith, I have a friend who was just telling me about a house that he purchased in Ross. I'll give him a call and see if he can recommend a realtor."

Within days, they were riding around in the back seat of a very fancy car with more bells and whistles than Meredith had even known existed. There were few homes for sale near town, as Larkspur had always been prime real estate. Their very officious realtor had three options that she thought might fit their needs nicely. Meredith did not like her much, but could tell she knew what she was talking about. After all, Meredith wasn't looking for a friend; she was looking for a home.

"Here we are," the petite woman said, and spewed a barrage of particulars from whatever she had clipped to her folder.

"I know you mean well, but I think Alan and I would like to walk through alone, and just get a feel for the house. If we have any questions, we'll come find you."

Leaving Marin's most sought-after realtor on the front porch, Alan and Meredith entered the foyer of house number one.

"Nicely done, babe," Alan said. He shook his head and chuckled, clearly getting a kick out of Meredith's spunk.

They toured all three homes and felt nothing for any of them. They decided that they could continue living as they were until something came on the market that suited them. They were not too concerned; they would be spending much of the summer at their beach house, anyway.

"What time do your parents arrive tomorrow?"

"They arrive late afternoon, but they are planning to spend a week in the city before joining us at the beach. I'm actually glad, because it will give me a few days to polish my final chapter before emailing it to Spencer. It will be such a relief to be finished. Honestly, all I want to do is spend a few weeks doing nothing but enjoying the family and lounging on the beach."

Alan was thrilled at the prospect of hosting Meredith's parents. Sadly, he had lost his mother to cancer as a child, and he'd had a strained relationship with his father ever since. The idea of a close-knit family appealed to him immensely. "Me too, sweetie."

Friday night they picked up the keys and arrived in time to stock the kitchen and make sure everything was in order. It was more beautiful than they had hoped, and they could not wait for Meredith's parents to arrive.

"Finally, Poppy is down. Wine?"

"Sure. On the deck?"

"Perfect," Meredith said.

They sat on the massive deck overlooking the spectacular Pacific Ocean, appreciating how lucky they both felt after experiencing such a tumultuous few months.

Chapter 46

Meredith proudly emailed Spencer the last chapter of her first book after rising early and finishing it in a sunny spot, which also offered up a 180-degree view of the ocean. She took a moment to truly reflect on how far she had come, and how much she had learned in the last year about her own strength and endurance.

"Hey, sweetie. You're up early," Alan said, shielding his eyes from the bright California sun.

"I just finished! Sent the final chapter to Spencer, so I am officially on vacation," she said, and leaned back in her chair with total satisfaction.

"Congratulations! Let's celebrate by walking down and having brunch at the Parkside Cafe. Best eggs Benedict around."

"Yum! I'll get Poppy up and be ready in ten minutes."

As they strolled down the quiet beach road, Alan announced that he intended to camp out on the beach all day and read her novel cover to cover.

"Well, there's not technically a cover yet, but you are welcome to my iPad," Meredith said with a smile.

After a terrific brunch, Meredith and Poppy zipped into the city to pick up her parents. Kissing Alan goodbye, Meredith promised to return in time for an early supper. He stood at the end of the driveway and watched until they were no longer in sight. It melted Alan's heart every time Poppy blew kisses and waved bye-bye. He knew she would need a father figure growing up, and was thrilled to fill the role. She had even called him dada the other day, which totally shocked both Meredith and Alan. Neither had corrected her; in fact, both of them felt at peace with it. Nobody would ever replace Peter, and they fully intended to show her pictures and tell her what a wonderful man he'd been when she was old enough to assimilate his tragic death.

After observing from their deck the hordes of people who had descended upon Stinson Beach to escape a typical foggy June day in San Francisco, Alan opted to stay at the house and read in solitude. It did not come as a shock that Meredith was a gifted writer. But he was surprised at how compelling the story line was, and he felt certain that it could easily be morphed into a script. He took copious notes as he pored over the impeccable text, and could not wait until they could carve out some time away from the family so they could discuss some ideas that could potentially allow them to work as colleagues.

When the car pulled in, Alan greeted Dr. and Mrs. Singler and assisted them with their bags. In the course of one week, Grace Singler had managed to do a significant amount of damage in the city. She took joy in showering her only granddaughter with clothes, books, and toys. While Meredith did not love the idea of spoiling Poppy, she didn't see any real harm in a few trinkets every once in a while. Although when she surveyed the arsenal of presents, Meredith kindly asked her mother not to bestow any more treasures for the duration of the trip.

Feeling very comfortable with Meredith's parents, Alan said, "Allow me to give you the grand tour and show you to your suite. I think you will find it very comfortable."

Meredith gave Poppy a quick supper and put the sleepy tot down for the night. It had been a busy day, and she was pleased to finally relax, joining the rest of the group on the deck while they admired the stellar view.

"I'll be right back," Alan said, ducking into the kitchen. He was chilling a bottle of his favorite champagne so they could announce their engagement with a toast.

"What's this?" Meredith's mother said.

Alan passed out four flutes of chilled Cristal, and he and Meredith raised their glasses and happily announced their plans to marry. Thrilled for both, Dr. and Mrs. Singler welled up, enthusiastically giving a hearty blessing to the union of a very deserving couple.

"We couldn't be happier for the two of you," Dr. Singler said, with a handshake for his future son-in-law, followed by a huge hug for his beautiful daughter.

"You know, Alan, you can thank me. The day we first met you at Rulli's, I told Meredith you fancied her," Grace Singler said in a self-satisfied tone.

"Well, thank you very much! Maybe I should give you the diamond ring that your daughter doesn't seem to want," Alan said with a raised eyebrow.

"What? Is this true, Meredith?" her mother said in disbelief.

"I'm just not a big-diamond-ring sort of gal. You know me, Mom."

"Well," Alan said. "I know this is not customary, but I thought you might like this."

From his pocket Alan pulled the most exquisite ring, a sapphire flanked with two beautiful diamonds. Clearly an antique, it looked like something a royal would wear.

"Alan, it is beautiful. Wh—where . . . ?"

"Ah, the lady is finally speechless," he said, making eye contact with her parents.

Meredith pulled herself together. "This is absolutely, without a doubt, the most stunning piece of jewelry I have ever seen in my entire life."

"It actually belonged to my great-grandmother. It was typically passed down to the women in the family. My mother's sister gave it to me last year before she died, and told me to give it to the woman of my dreams. Meredith, you are the woman of my dreams."

Shaking slightly, she allowed Alan to slip it onto her finger. The fit was perfect, but it was the thought that meant more to Meredith than anything else she had ever received.

Not a dry eye on the deck, they polished off the bottle. Then they brought out some appetizers to nibble while catching up on the latest news from Portland. Little was said about Meredith's recent scare. Her parents had exhausted the topic after it occurred and did not see any need to revisit it again. Dr. and Mrs. Singler had each separately thanked Alan for handling the situation and remaining strong for their daughter.

They all felt happy and satisfied after a lovely steak dinner coupled with a bottle of wine from Alan's impressive collection. The sunset was especially beautiful, and they all agreed to spend the following day enjoying a lazy afternoon at the beach.

After retiring to their private quarters, Alan pulled Meredith close and made love to her quietly. They fell asleep after a special day both would always remember. Meredith had the approval of her parents, which was important to her. But more importantly, Alan had told her he felt as though he was now part of a real family—something he had not known, but had been hungry for since he was a boy.

Chapter 47

*A*lan and Meredith woke before the others and took the opportunity to enjoy a pot of coffee in the sunroom overlooking the beach. It was foggy and cool but the fog would likely burn off, giving them another brilliant day.

"So, I read your book while you were in the city yesterday."

"The whole thing?"

"Meredith, and I am not just saying this: it is one of the best I have seen in a long time."

"Really? Are you sure you're not a little biased?"

"Seriously, I love it so much that I would like your permission to give a copy to a really talented filmmaker, who I know would agree with me."

Meredith looked at Alan in disbelief, but her stunned expression soon became a huge smile, which gave way to the infectious giggle that always made him laugh out loud.

"I will give it to you," she said, "on one condition."

"Lay it on me."

"I will only put my seal of approval on a movie that is directed by a woman."

"Well, that's easy then, because the person I am thinking of happens to be one of the best directors in the business, and she is a woman," Alan said with pride.

"Really?"

"Well, I haven't seen her for a few years, but right after I finished my first film, I met her at one of those stuffy awards shows. Of course, she had no clue who I was at the time, but she was incredibly kind and generous. When my film was finally released, she sent me a congratulatory note, suggesting that we collaborate at some point. Honestly, Meredith, I think this project would knock her socks off!"

"Who is it?"

"Oh, right. Kate Simmons."

"You mean the smartest and most creative female director of all time, Kate Simmons?"

"Uh-huh."

"You mean two-time-Oscar-winning Kate Simmons?"

"That's the one."

"Holy shit, Alan!"

Laughing, he pulled her close and looked straight into her eyes. "Your book is that good, Meredith."

His faith in her work was such an incredible compliment, and Meredith could tell he was being honest. She looked over the notes he'd taken and was blown away by the fact that they shared the same basic vision for the characters, as well as the tone and energy of the story.

Meredith elected not to prematurely say anything to her parents for fear that it could jinx the whole thing. Instead, she put the thoughts of collaborating professionally with Alan aside and enjoyed a terrific day on the beach, playing in the sand and dipping Poppy's toes in the cold water until she squealed with delight. That night they dined on Meredith's famous made-from-scratch pizza and a huge salad.

"There's nothing like pizza and a beer," Dr. Singler said, visibly relaxed. Poppy sat comfortably on his lap, fighting the urge to fall asleep.

"I'll second that," Alan said.

Meredith and her mother took the sleepy tot inside and put her to bed before she conked out in her grandfather's arms. Meredith also wanted to give Alan some time alone with her dad. They had really hit it off and seemed to talk with little effort about subjects that they both enjoyed.

"Honey, your dad and I could not be happier. Do you have a wedding date set?" Grace said, admiring the ring Alan had presented to her daughter the previous evening.

"No, but it won't be big. We have both had the traditional wedding, and neither of us has any interest in making a production of it."

"Makes sense."

"Actually, I really just want to go to city hall, get married, and call it a day."

"Meredith, I think you should! You can always have a party to celebrate afterward. Besides, you and Alan have both been through a rough couple of years. Why wait and create more headaches with the stress of planning a formal event?"

"I have to say, Mom, it's tempting. Any interest in babysitting tomorrow while we sneak into the city and get married?"

"We have absolutely no place to be, and we'd love to," Grace Singler said, clapping her hands.

That night, after Meredith and Alan slipped into bed, she rolled over and said, "Wanna get married?"

"I thought we already nailed that down," he said, kissing her neck.

"No, I mean, do you want to get married tomorrow at city hall? I've lined up a babysitter and everything," she said coyly.

As he pulled her nightgown over her head, Meredith said, "I'll take that as a yes."

Chapter 48

The next morning, Dr. and Mrs. Singler waved goodbye as the happy couple drove into the city to make their union official. While it seemed a bit spontaneous, both Alan and Meredith felt like it was right, and they laughed all the way. Poppy was perfectly happy to remain at home, playing with her doting grandparents at the beach and napping happily in a makeshift bed on the shady side of the deck after lunch.

San Francisco City Hall was one of the most beautiful buildings in the Bay Area, known for its historical significance. Both Alan and Meredith felt it was an honor to recite their vows within its grand architecture. Before the honorable judge, under the massive dome of the rotunda, they promised to love and cherish each other for the rest of their lives. Without a bit of hesitation, they sealed their commitment with a kiss, knowing in their hearts they were meant to be together always. The wedding took less than ten minutes, but the perfection of the simple service suited them well.

They walked hand in hand down the street and stopped at a fancy bakery, where they shared a red velvet cupcake to commemorate their nuptials.

"So I was thinking, Mrs. Harrison, any chance we can convince your mother to come back in August so we can take a real honeymoon?"

"First, I love being called Mrs. Harrison. And second, all she can do is say no, which I highly doubt."

They drove back to Stinson Beach, admiring the fiery red sunset as they pulled into town. They were husband and wife, and it had happened without the hassle of any wedding-planning headaches. As they walked up the front steps, Alan scooped Meredith up. He carried her right over the threshold and into the living room, where a serious tower of blocks was being erected by Dr. Singler while Poppy and her adoring grandmother looked on.

It was an unconventional wedding night, but they toasted with mimosas and feasted on stacks of blueberry pancakes and crispy bacon.

"First wedding ever with breakfast on the menu," Alan said, flipping his wife another pancake and a wink.

"We can have a bash later. For today, this is perfect," Meredith said. She felt incredibly blessed.

"So, Grace, Meredith and I were wondering if we could convince you to spend a few weeks in August with Poppy here at Stinson Beach. If you prefer, you could even go back and forth between the Larkspur and Stinson houses. We would love to take a honeymoon before I begin work on my film in the fall. If you were unaware, I happen to be married to a woman who spent like a billion dollars on a fancy European extravaganza at an auction for dogs," Alan said, with a hint of humorous disapproval.

"Don't get me started, Alan. I said the same thing to her," Dr. Singler said from across the room.

"Um, excuse me, but if you want to be invited on that first-class trip, you would be wise to lose the attitude!" Meredith said, hands on her hips.

They all laughed. Alan especially got a kick out of her as she got all worked up about it. While he loved riling her up, he actually fell head over heels in love with her that night, and never quite got over her incredible generosity.

Outside, the fog rolled in. Dr. and Mrs. Singler gave the baby a bath and put her to bed so Alan and Meredith could enjoy a cozy romantic evening. They sat in front of the fireplace planning their honeymoon and then retired to their suite, exhausted but not too tired to properly consummate their marriage. Drifting off to sleep, both declared how grateful they felt to be able to spend the rest of their lives together.

Chapter 49

The rest of the summer flew by, and before too long they were in the final stages of planning their trip. They decided to fly into Venice, then to Milan for a whirlwind shopping adventure. From there they would make their way to Portofino, where they would board a private chartered yacht, ending their spectacular holiday in Capri. It was sure to be the vacation of a lifetime.

With two weeks to go until they left, Alan called Meredith from Los Angeles, where he was meeting with his production team one last time before leaving for Europe. Meredith was in Larkspur trying to tie up loose ends.

"What's up?" he said. He had just finished his last meeting while checking his watch to see if he could make an earlier flight to San Francisco.

"Trying to get Poppy and my mom squared away so they don't have to do much while we're gone. How was your meeting?"

"Good. Everything is moving forward as planned, and we are set to begin shooting in mid-September. Say, have you ever been to the Outside Lands Music Festival in the city?"

"No, but I've always wanted to go!"

"Well, my lovely bride, this is your lucky day. I have two VIP tickets for tomorrow night. What are the chances that Kathryn could watch our little Poppy?"

"I'll ask. See you when you get home."

Kathryn was thrilled to babysit Poppy, and she shooed them out the door as quickly as possible. It was a perfectly warm summer evening after a morning of fog and rain. When they arrived, the concert was well underway. As they located their luxury cabana with a perfect view of the stage, Meredith impressively mouthed the words along with the tatted-up lead singer of Metallica.

"How is it that I am married to a metal head and had no fucking idea?" Alan said, secretly turned on.

Ignoring him, she continued singing.

"Please tell me you don't put Poppy to bed with that song."

"No, she much prefers Ozzy," Meredith said, laughing.

They returned home that night thoroughly fulfilled. They had seen every performer from Stevie Wonder to the Red Hot Chili Peppers and had vowed to return the following year. But for now they had a trip to prepare for; they could not wait to spend two glorious weeks alone in Italy.

The day before they left for Europe, Alan received an urgent call from their realtor.

"Mr. Harrison, you need to come right away. I am almost certain your dream house has come on the market. Problem is it's everyone's dream house, so you and Meredith had better move fast."

"Where is it? I can meet you there right now."

Alan called Meredith, who was on her way home from picking her mother up at the airport, and gave her the exciting news.

"I'll be there as soon as I can," Meredith said. She was a little frustrated by the timing, as they were leaving the country in less than twenty-four hours. But she also knew that if their realtor was that emphatic about the property, it must be good.

Two hours later they walked away having offered full price for the pristine property, located just two blocks from the center of town. It had all the specifications they'd requested. It was basically the bungalow, but it had three additional bedrooms, a huge den, a formal dining room, and a sunny space over the garage that Alan said they could easily convert to an art studio for Meredith.

"I cannot believe how effortlessly our lives have fallen into place. How is it that we are so lucky, Alan?"

"When it's meant to be, it will be," he said, kissing her.

It was difficult for Meredith to leave Poppy, but she knew she would be in good hands with her mother. Sitting in the first-class airport lounge, Meredith checked her email before their flight departed.

"Oh my gosh, my book is officially hitting the shelves on November first. They want me to do a three-week book tour from the end of October to the middle of November."

"I am so proud of you, Meredith."

Smiling from ear to ear, Meredith said, "I have to be honest, it's becoming very real, very fast!"

Landing in Italy was surreal. They drank wine, ate amazing food, and, of course, made love all the time. They were especially pleased that their public displays of affection were commonplace; the locals were not at all shocked or offended by overt sexual behavior.

"I could get used to this, Meredith," Alan said, nuzzling her ear and kissing her proudly on the streets of Milan.

"Can't say I mind it either," she said with her classic giggle.

By the second week, they were happy to board their private yacht and make their way to picturesque Capri, an island that had historically beckoned celebrities and international royalty. Meredith had always wanted to go, and it did not disappoint. They spent their days discovering local markets that offered up specialties of the island—perfume for Meredith's mom, handmade sandals for Poppy, and an exquisite pottery bowl for Kathryn. They also sent two cases of the island's famous limoncello back home so Alan could dole it out to colleagues on the set of his upcoming film. After sunny days full of shopping and lunching on Italian delicacies, they took a small boat back to their yacht, which was anchored a short distance from shore.

Their deck was perfectly shielded from onlookers, and the last night they made love under the stars. As they nestled together under a blanket in the cool evening breeze, Alan told Meredith again how privileged he felt to become a father figure to Poppy.

"I never want to take anything from Peter, because he will always be her father, Meredith. But if and when you are ready, I would love nothing more than to adopt Poppy. I just want her to know how much I love her, and I want her to feel that she is a part of this family."

Meredith kissed Alan through her tears. It meant so much to her. She immediately accepted, saying that she would contact her lawyer right away to move the adoption process forward.

The two glorious weeks in Italy would always hold special memories for Alan and Meredith, but they also looked forward to returning home and beginning their life together in Larkspur.

Chapter 50

At the end of the week, Meredith's mother returned home, having thoroughly enjoyed her time with Poppy. Things were progressing nicely with the new house. The inspection revealed a few small issues, but nothing that could not be negotiated and repaired prior to closing. They were tentatively set to move in on the first of September, which would give them two weeks to get settled before Alan began work on his new film. Amazingly, his home sold before it hit the market, to a couple who had previously said they wanted the first opportunity to look if he ever wanted to sell.

"I've arranged for the movers to pack both of our houses beginning on the twenty-fifth, so we can move in on the first," Alan told Meredith, as Poppy splashed around in the bath.

"Good. I think I might be coming down with something. I am just not myself this week."

"Sweetie, we have had a crazy few months. Take it easy today while I'm at work so we can go to bed early, if you know what I mean," Alan said, and kissed his wife goodbye.

As the day went on, Meredith had a sinking feeling that she knew what the culprit was, and she scrambled for her calendar.

"Oh, shit," she said, and laughed out loud. A quick trip to the pharmacy confirmed what she suspected. She was pregnant. By chance, her doctor had an opening and was able to fit her in at noon. Kathryn was happy to take Poppy for the afternoon, believing Meredith when she said that she had a few last-minute errands to run before the move.

"I'm going to have a baby, aren't I?"

"Meredith, you are partially right."

"Dr. Blackwell, how can I be partially pregnant?"

"You were correct about being pregnant. But it's not a baby. It's babies, Meredith. My dear, there are two strong heartbeats, and I would put your progress at about four weeks."

After a bout of hysterical laughter, she thanked the doctor, and ventured home in a bit of a haze. She did not tell Kathryn, as she wanted Alan to be the first to know. But she needed to find the perfect way to tell him the big news.

That evening after they put Poppy to bed, she gave Alan two small boxes. Inside the first box was a silver frame with a photo of Poppy and Alan on Stinson Beach. They were playing in the sand, and both were laughing. It was a terrific picture, one of Meredith's favorites. Inside the other box, she had placed two more silver frames. In lieu of photos, she had simply placed a card in each. One said "Baby #1"; the other, "Baby #2."

When it finally dawned on Alan, he smiled through the tears that streamed down his face. He had endured so much loss, and now he had a beautiful wife, a daughter, and two more on the way. So much to be grateful for, so much to look forward to.

"We got our basketball team, Meredith," he said, and kissed her slowly.

By mid-September the house was miraculously in order and Meredith's queasy stomach was on the mend as long as she was equipped at all times with saltines and ginger tea. Alan felt ambivalent about leaving Meredith and Poppy to spend the week in Los Angeles working on the film. But Meredith was not concerned at all. She had lots to do in their new home and wanted to complete her to-do list by the time she left on her book tour. Besides, Poppy loved her play dates, and Meredith did not want to disrupt her schedule by flying back and forth.

Alan arrived home Friday night, having luckily caught the last shuttle from LAX. He looked exhausted, and said he could not wait to do nothing all weekend long.

"How's the filming going?" Meredith said, pouring him a glass of wine, as she sipped her ginger tea.

"Good. Everything seems to be going swimmingly. I just hope that it is not a precursor to a postproduction nightmare."

"Don't say that, Alan!"

"I also have a bit of good news to share with you, Meredith."

"Oh?"

Just then Meredith's cell rang. It was Kathryn, wanting to know if she could drop by.

"Sure, come on over."

Within two minutes there was a knock at the door, and on the porch stood Kathryn, holding the most adorable chocolate-brown fluff ball Meredith had ever seen.

"Oh my gosh, I wish Poppy was awake to see this little cutie pie! Come in, come in!"

Kathryn entered the house with a huge smile on her face. Alan heard the commotion and waved both women into the family room.

"Who is this?" Alan said.

"I don't know. You tell me," Kathryn said with a mischievous look.

When Alan and Meredith stopped laughing and snuggling the pup, Kathryn reminded her what she had said several months before.

"You told me that if the shelter ever received a Labradoodle, you had dibs on it. Well, this is your lucky day. She is actually a fancy-pants Australian Labradoodle from Rhode Island. This couple from Mill Valley intended to take possession of her when she arrived—via private jet, thank you very much. At the last minute they had a family emergency and had to leave the country indefinitely. They called me in a panic this morning, and I told them I had the perfect home for her. Mer, she is a huge love, and I know she would fit perfectly with your family. Come on, look at this face! She could be your little family mascot!"

Meredith and Alan looked at each other and shook their heads. It was impulsive, but she was irresistible, and neither could say no. Besides, they now had a huge backyard where the puppy could play with the kiddos.

"Well, what's her name gonna be?" Kathryn said.

"It's up to you, Meredith. You can pick this one," Alan said with a wink.

"I have always loved the name Vivian."

"Well, hello there, Vivian," Alan said. And the dog bounded across the room and plunked down right next to him like a big dust mop. They all laughed. Clearly she was going to make a fine addition to their already chaotic household.

"Thank you, Kathryn," Meredith said, giving her friend a huge hug.

"Are you crazy, Mer? It's the least I could do, after everything you have done for me and your incredible support of the foundation."

Alan and Meredith spent the evening falling madly in love with Vivian. She looked as though she had a big Hershey's kiss for a nose, and she peered through her curly brown locks with the most adoring eyes.

"You realize Poppy is going to flip when she wakes up in the morning," Meredith said, clapping her hands.

"She's not the only one," Alan said with a sneaky smile.

"What do you mean?" Meredith said nervously. She didn't know if she could handle another surprise that evening.

"Well, just before Vivian waltzed into our lives, I was about to tell you that I had a very encouraging lunch today."

"Oh?" Meredith said, in mid-snuggle with the pup.

"Yep."

"Well, out with it. Don't just sit there and keep a pregnant lady waiting!"

"I didn't want to prematurely tell you in case it didn't pan out, but I had a two-hour lunch with a very excited, very animated Kate Simmons. Not only did she read your book, she absolutely fell in love with it. Meredith, she basically gave you and me carte blanche to write a script that she said she would be proud to direct."

"Are you kidding?"

"Nope. And not only that, she has three A-listers who are very interested in executive-producing and have said they would love to financially back the project."

Standing motionless, overwhelmed by the events of the evening, Meredith said, "Alan, that kind of filmmaking doesn't exist in today's world."

"Well, it's happening. I would say your first call in the morning should be to Spencer, because your book is going to be a huge success with the buzz of a movie on its heels."

"This is the most exciting news," Meredith said, unable to wipe the huge grin from her face.

Once they got Miss Vivian to sleep, they finally settled down and fell into bed. Meredith slid close to Alan, whispering very naughty things in his ear.

"Such dirty talk from an expectant mother," he said, pulling her shirt off.

"How do you think I got this way?"

They fell asleep in each other's arms after a most pleasurable ending for both.

The next morning was a burst of excitement. When Poppy and Vivian officially met, it was love at first sight. They all spent a lazy weekend becoming better acquainted. They took Vivian to Rulli's, where they sat outside, and began teaching her proper puppy etiquette. Between Poppy's curly locks and Vivian, who was a burst of puppy magic, the Harrison family received a lot of attention from passersby.

By Sunday evening they were reenergized, looking forward to a fresh week. Sadly, Alan would have to leave on Monday afternoon to be in Los Angeles for the duration of the week, but it wasn't forever. Plus, they knew that the following project would be a family affair.

"So, when will you be finished filming?" Meredith asked.

"They are moving quickly, so my guess is the end of October. Postproduction will resume after the first of the year, but we will have a few months before it gets crazy again."

"My mom has generously agreed to join me on the book tour to watch Poppy, and Kathryn begged me to let her take Vivian. Maybe you could join us for the tail end of the trip. I'll make it worth your while," she said, intentionally throaty and seductive.

From across the room, he gave her the smile and single eyebrow lift that still managed to give her butterflies.

Chapter 51

*J*ust as Alan suspected, the movie was completed without a hitch, and by November first he joined his family in New York City. Then on to Chicago, Dallas, and Seattle, finishing in Meredith's hometown of Portland, Oregon. She looked forward to showing Alan around and introducing him to her friends.

Meredith arrived in Portland as a best-selling author and was received as something of a celebrity. A sizable article was splashed across the front page of the paper, and a local morning show was thrilled that she'd agreed to do an interview. They stayed a few extra days with her parents in order to give Alan the true flavor of their quirky Northwest town. Naturally, it was somewhat difficult to revisit the streets of Portland, as the city still held so many sad memories for Meredith. But seeing friends and introducing them to Alan more than made up for the distant remembrance of her previous life.

As their plane touched down in San Francisco, Alan and Meredith could not wait to get home and take a well-deserved respite. The year had had so many highs, and now they wanted to take a break and fly under the radar for a while.

The holidays were magical, and Meredith was well into her second trimester. Her book remained on the best-seller list, and everything was falling into place, with the movie set to begin filming the following year.

Just before New Year's, Alan came home from his daily run with a bit of a spring in his step. Meredith knew immediately that he had something to tell her, and he was obviously going to torture her before letting the cat out of the bag.

"All right, out with it," she said, folding her arms and shifting from side to side in an effort to hurry her husband along.

"Guess who I just ran into?"

"Who?"

"Remember that guy I introduced you to at Kathryn's gala last year? The one from the tech company?"

"Sort of."

"Well, I'm not sure I told you, but he was in town while you were on your book tour, and I invited him over one night for drinks. Seems that he was quite enamored with your art. He wants to commission you to do a painting," Alan said, trying to contain his excitement.

"What? That's too much pressure. What if he hates it?"

"What are you talking about, Meredith? Just talk to him."

"What's his name again?"

"Collin Andrews. Oh, and by the way, we are meeting him at Lark Creek for dinner tonight. I already arranged for Kathryn to come over and babysit Poppy and Vivian. All you have to do is show up and be your spectacular self," he said, kissing her neck.

She was always weak when he did that, and this time was no exception. Her sex drive was off the charts now that she was in her second trimester, and Alan was not complaining. By the time Poppy got up from her much-needed nap, they had made love once in bed and again in the shower.

Meredith smiled as she pulled on a new maternity dress that her mother had sent her. She knew it was expensive because it was from the Stella McCartney line. But she figured she needed to look smashing, and she did. Looking in the mirror, she caught the eye of her husband. He was grinning proudly, enthusiastically giving her the thumbs-up.

"How is it possible that you are more and more sexy every day?"

"We'll see if you're still saying that in a few months," she said, rolling her eyes.

It was a perfect evening, so they decided to walk to dinner. They made a beautiful couple, and heads always turned when they were together. They were so obviously in love, and it showed in the way that they looked at each other. When they entered the restaurant, Collin approached them immediately and introduced himself to Meredith again. He was a lovely man, and they all enjoyed a great dinner on the deck.

"Okay, Meredith. I would like to know why it is that you have kept your painting under wraps," Collin said, shaking his finger at her playfully.

"What can I say, Collin, I'm a writer who happens to paint as a hobby."

"Well, it seems to me you should be a writer who is also one of Marin's up-and-coming artists. Let me cut to the chase. I want to purchase a painting similar to the one that hangs over your fireplace. It is perfect for my house in Malibu, and you can basically name your price. I guarantee, though, that once I hang it, you will have a slew of clients."

Meredith could not fathom what he had just told her. She felt excited, yet nervous. It was the creative part of her that she never liked to talk about very much, and she honestly did not know how she felt about selling her art. It seemed a little like she was selling her soul.

"Tell you what, Collin. I'll think about it and get back to you."

"That's fair. When you're ready, just know that there will be an open space ready for your masterpiece."

The men toasted the evening with champagne, while Meredith drank Pellegrino. While some women justified a little alcohol during pregnancy, Meredith adhered to a strict no-booze, no-caffeine rule. She did not see the need to take any chances.

Walking home, Alan and Meredith strolled hand in hand, chatting about the evening's events. It was still shocking to Meredith, but Alan was not at all surprised.

"I cannot tell you how proud I am of you, Meredith. First thing in the morning I am going to call our contractor and have that room over the garage finished so you have a proper studio."

"Well, if I'm going to do this, I suppose I need a place to do it," she said, shaking her head in disbelief.

Chapter 52

The next two weeks flew by and it was time for Alan to resume his trips to Los Angeles, to work on the postproduction portion of his film. They had an enormous amount of editing to do in order to release it as a summer blockbuster. The days were grueling, and he could not wait to get home on Friday evenings to rejuvenate.

Meredith was getting bigger and bigger. She had four weeks to go and could not wait until the babies arrived. She and Alan had decided to hold off on finding out the sex of the twins. They had agreed upon a short list of names but wanted to meet the newest family members before deciding. Both Alan and Meredith hoped he would be finished with postproduction, but it was going to be close. Meredith filled her time morphing her book into a script that they would be proud to take to the executive producers, who were anxiously awaiting the finished product. She also began dabbling in her new art studio, which had the most perfect light. She had never felt so inspired to paint and had recently begun work on Collin's painting in her free time.

"Meredith, this is beyond fantastic," Alan said, reading the script one Saturday morning. "It's as if you have always written for film. Is there anything you can't do?" He put it aside briefly to pull his wife closer.

"As a matter of fact, there is. I can no longer fit into my clothes," she said in her classic sarcastic tone.

"I disagree, Meredith. You look amazing in and out of your clothes!"

They spent a quiet weekend taking walks with Poppy and Vivian and enjoying their beautiful home. The time seemed to fly by, and soon Alan was kissing Meredith goodbye before he departed for another week.

Kathryn asked if she could have Poppy for the day, as they were expecting a bunch of baby bunnies at the shelter. Meredith knew Poppy would love it, and figured she could make a nice dent in Collin's painting. The day flew by, and before she knew it Poppy was bounding into her studio very excited, chatting nonstop about the bunnies that she'd met during the course of her day.

"Holy crap, Meredith, I am totally blown away by that painting!"

"Thanks, Kathryn. I am really pleased with the way it's coming together."

"Who are you painting it for?"

"Actually, it's my first commissioned piece, for a guy Alan knows."

"Well, whoever he is, he's going to love it!"

"Hey, Kathryn, I made a huge pot of chicken noodle soup. Stay and have dinner with Poppy and me."

"I'd love to, but I have a date tonight."

"Do tell!"

"He's that guy I met at the Mill Valley Film Festival in October."

"I remember him. Why have I not heard more about him?"

"I don't know. Honestly, I don't think I am marriage material."

"That's ridiculous! You are absolutely marriage material, Kathryn."

"Well, I may not be marriage-worthy, but he is awesome in bed, and that's my plan for tonight!"

"Good for you, Kathryn. Now get out of here and go get laid!"

As Kathryn left, Meredith laughed to herself. She loved her friend, but secretly thought that she sabotaged her relationships on purpose because she genuinely loved being unattached and did not want to be told what to do.

"The eternal bachelorette," Meredith said to herself, watching Kathryn run down the back stairs.

Chapter 53

Meredith couldn't wait for Alan to arrive home on Friday. As her due date neared, she was beginning to feel more and more anxious. The film was nearly complete, but she would not be totally content until he was back for good.

"Hello, I'm home."

Poppy squealed at the sound of his voice. She scrambled into his arms, going on and on about the bunnies she had seen with Kathryn at the shelter. Meredith was close behind, held back by the babies, who were officially beginning to slow her down.

"How is my stunningly beautiful wife?" Alan said, pulling her close and fondling her backside.

"She is huge!"

"She is sexy."

"Alan, you always know just what to say to a girl."

Poppy was in her pajamas and ready for bed. Alan deposited his bag in the foyer and happily put her to bed with her three favorite books. By the time her bedroom door clicked shut, she was already down for the count.

"Are you hungry?"

"Yes, for you," he said, unbuttoning her blouse.

"You know what they say about sex this close to the due date, Alan."

"I don't care, because the film is complete," he whispered in her ear.

"Are you serious?"

"I wasn't sure, and I didn't want to get your hopes up. I am happy to say there will be no more trips to Los Angeles for a while."

They had missed being adventurous over the last few months, but they felt like they could indulge now that Alan was home for good. Even in her final month, Meredith was amorous, and she could not get enough of Alan. He showed that he felt the same way about her as they made up for lost time.

"Better get your fill now. Once these babies come, it's going to be mayhem around here," Meredith said as she initiated a little kicker sex romp.

"Well, if I must," he said, with a dramatic, stone-faced shrug.

They made love again, thrilled that they would finally be able to live together full-time. Both famished, they ventured into the kitchen to make scrambled eggs and toast.

"Hey, I started Collin's painting while you were gone. Run up to the studio and take a look at it while I finish up here. I really want to know what you think."

Alan was in the studio for what seemed like a very long time to Meredith. By the wide grin on his face, he was clearly impressed with her newest piece.

"Meredith, it's fantastic! The energy and flow of your work never ceases to amaze me. Collin is going to love it! Have you given any thought to what you are going to charge?"

"I have no clue. What do you think?"

"I'd say five thousand dollars."

"That's nuts, Alan!"

"Meredith, he is an art collector. I am sure it won't even faze him. In fact, he will probably think it's a steal."

"Honestly, I don't know. I'm going to have to give this more thought."

They spent the rest of the evening in front of the fireplace, noshing on eggs and toast and watching an old episode of their favorite drama series on television.

Now that Alan was home for good, they both looked forward to working full-time on the film. Meredith had completed a good portion in his absence, and Alan had very few changes. They worked very well as a team and respected each other's creativity and individual writing styles.

Meredith wanted to finish Collin's painting before the babies came, knowing that she would have very little spare time once she was caring for three little ones. All she had to do was finish the olives in the martini glass, and she would be done. A few days later, she finally completed her first commissioned piece. She stood back, changed a few minor details, and then added her signature. She was very proud of the finished product and felt confident that her first client would like it.

"Wow! He is going to be ecstatic when he sees this," Alan said, entering Meredith's art studio as she surveyed the final product.

"I am going to call him in the morning and let him know he can arrange to have it crated and delivered to his home in Malibu. I have this gut feeling that I am getting close to delivering these little ones. I've felt kind of queasy all day."

"What? I wish you would have said something. Why don't you lie down, and I will make you some tea."

Smiling at her adoring husband, she said, "You are so good to me, Alan. I think I will take you up on that offer."

They spent a quiet evening at home and retired early. A few hours later Meredith woke to a familiar feeling. Her water had broken, and she was beginning to have those very memorable labor pains.

"This is it," Alan said. "We're about to get our basketball team."

They called Kathryn, who was happily on standby to mind Poppy and Vivian. She came over right away, and off they went to the hospital. Meredith was a trooper. She managed to push both babies out, though she was not too proud to accept the epidural that was offered to her by her doctor. For some reason they were totally surprised yet thrilled that they had a boy and a girl. Both babies weighed in at around six and a half pounds and were healthy as could be.

"Okay, Mom, what's it going to be?" Alan said, holding their short list of names.

"Let's go with our top picks from both lists."

"Done," Alan said.

When Kathryn entered the room with Poppy, Meredith was simultaneously nursing both babies with some guidance from a nurse.

"Who do we have here?" Kathryn said. There were tears in her eyes.

"This is Jack Riley, and this is Sophie Anne."

"Meredith, they are beautiful. I cannot believe how good you look after pushing two little footballs out this morning!"

"I am not going to lie to you, Kathryn, I am exhausted. But it was so worth it. Now, come here, my little Poppy girl."

Meredith patted the bed, encouraging the tot to join her. They all sat together, and Kathryn took a few pictures, to capture the memory of Poppy and the babies meeting for the very first time.

Alan came into the room, and Poppy screamed with excitement. He scooped her up and gave her a big kiss. The babies did not even flinch when she let out a burst of audible joy, and Meredith laughed to herself, thinking that they were probably used to her high-pitched squeals after nine months in utero.

"Good news, everyone. I just spoke with the doctor, and we can go home as early as tomorrow."

"That's great!" Meredith said.

The nurse could see that Meredith was growing weary and took the liberty of transporting the babies to the nursery so she could get a little sleep. Kathryn followed suit and said, "Give your mommy a smooch, Miss Poppy. We are heading out for an early supper and story time at the Book Passage in Corte Madera. It's going to be two gals out on the town this evening." The local cafe and bookstore had a stellar reputation for its gourmet menu options. But more importantly, it was known for stocking the finest selection of current must-read novels. Poppy, of course, always made a beeline for the kiddo section, where any and all of the year's award-winning children's literature could be found. They always had a terrific time, and never left with any less than an armful of bedtime treasures.

Meredith smiled and waved goodbye. She watched her daughter's blond curls bounce away. Maybe it was the hormones, but tears streamed down her cheeks while she reflected on how blissfully happy she felt after the birth of Jack and Sophie. After all, her last experience had come with so many conflicting feelings.

"Are you okay, sweetie?" Alan said.

"Yes. I am just so lucky to have such an amazing family, Alan."

He kissed her cheek and ordered her to sleep. She smiled, closed her eyes, and drifted off to dream of her blessed life.

Chapter 54

By the time the babies reached six weeks old, the whole family seemed to have fallen into a nice routine. The little ones slept well, only waking up once during the night. Poppy had finally come to terms with the fact that she now had to share her parents, and pleasantly discovered that being a big sister afforded her many privileges, like fetching diapers and assisting with bottle duty. Though she did have the occasional tantrum, she truly adored Jack and Sophie and looked forward to the day that they could be actual playmates.

Collin had the painting shipped to his home in Malibu, and he could not have been more pleased. He did not question the price for a moment. He told Meredith that she would likely have more interested customers after his annual Fourth of July bash.

As the deadline for the script loomed, Meredith became increasingly concerned. After putting Poppy down for the night, she said, "To be honest, Alan, I will be shocked if we complete this script in time. Frankly, I'm getting a little nervous. My parents are coming for two weeks, plus I promised Spencer I would send him a full outline for my second book by the end of the month."

"Tell you what, I will make a few calls and see if we can get an extension."

"They do that?"

"Well, it is not something I like to do often, but I don't see any harm in an extra sixty days or so."

"That would be perfect."

"All they can say is no."

Relieved, Meredith fed the babies and tucked them into their cribs for the night. She was exhausted and could not wait to fall into bed.

When she opened her eyes the next morning and saw that it was after nine, she jumped out of bed in a panic. But her fears were replaced with laughter when she spotted Alan and the three little ones happily eating breakfast on the patio. Alan had gotten them up and was feeding the babies with the reserve milk that Meredith pumped and stored in the freezer. Vivian was in her usual place under the table, anticipating that Poppy would likely drop her pancake at any moment.

"Well good morning, sunshine," Alan said. "Come join us for a little breakfast."

"Have I told you how much I love you?" Meredith said. She kissed all three of her kids, followed by an even bigger kiss for her amazing husband.

"Yes, but you can tell me again."

"I love you, Alan. And tonight I'm going to show you."

"I love a rested wife," he whispered, clearly proud of his morning accomplishments.

"I am not sure I told you, but my parents decided to rent a car, so we don't have to pick them up from the airport today. They should arrive around noon. We can walk to town for lunch, and then come back here so these little twerps can have a proper nap."

"Perfect! By the way, good news! We got a two-month extension from the studio. Turns out they were going to push it back anyway."

"I am so relieved. That will give us plenty of time to finish after my parents leave."

Meredith was thrilled to see her parents, and they were equally excited to meet the newest pair of family members.

"Oh, honey, they are absolutely adorable, and so good," her mother said as she cuddled Jack. Sophie was snoring happily in the arms of Dr. Singler, who had clearly fallen in love with his newest granddaughter. Poppy was dressed in her pink tutu and performing ballet for the group. They went to Rulli's and sat outside, eating a late lunch and catching up. Afterward, they made their way home and put all three kiddos to bed.

"Can I get you anything to drink?" Meredith said before they settled on the patio to relax.

"We're fine, sweetie. We do have some news, though."

"Good news, I hope."

"Well, it depends on how you look at it," Dr. Singler said.

"What do you mean?" Meredith said, concerned.

"Well, dear, we are moving to France."

"What?"

"Remember last year when we went to Paris? Well, your father met a colleague there who asked him if he would ever consider moving to Paris for a year, to take over his position while he took sabbatical. At the time, we didn't have any interest, but we have slowly come to the realization that it would be a wonderful opportunity."

"What are we talking about?" Alan said, joining them mid-conversation.

"My parents are moving to Paris for a year!"

"That's terrific! Good for you."

Grace Singler said, "We are actually getting very excited. It all happened so quickly, and with such ease. Kind of the way it happened for you, Meredith. I guess when it's meant to be, it will be."

After taking a moment to reconsider her initial reaction, Meredith said, "I am really happy for you. Where will you live?"

"We are renting a flat near the Left Bank. It is perfect walking distance to anything and everything. It will be *très magnifique!*"

They all laughed at Dr. Singler's animated French. While Meredith was going to miss having her parents so close, she knew they were deserving of this rich opportunity.

"When do you leave?" Alan said.

"Next month," they said in unison.

"Wow! Talk about a whirlwind decision," Meredith said.

Just then the babies started stirring, and Meredith realized that they had been chatting for almost two hours. Since everyone was tired, they ordered in, and celebrated with a bottle of their favorite wine. Meredith and Alan told her parents all about his film due out in the summer, and also about the script that they were in the process of completing for the following year. After a wonderful evening, Dr. and Mrs. Singler took the opportunity to remind their daughter how proud they were of the woman and mother she had become.

Chapter 55

Their visit went quickly, and before they knew it they were saying goodbye. It was especially difficult because Meredith knew it would be several months before she would see her parents again. As she waved, Alan reassured her by quietly grabbing her free hand. She knew they were going to have a spectacular year but could not imagine not seeing them for so long.

"Meredith, don't worry. We can take the family to Paris for a visit."

"Twin babies and a toddler?" she said, her eyes as big as dinner plates.

"Sure. I'm always up for a challenge!"

"We'll see."

They soon resumed their very ordinary schedule and found that the script was moving quicker than either expected. They settled into the flow of writing and found it inspiring to create the project together. They completed it with three weeks to spare, and agreed it had turned out to be a very special script. They knew the studio would love it. Neither wanted to jinx it, but it was one of those creative ventures that happened organically and resulted in an exceptional piece of writing. They were thrilled that they had several months before they would be needed on set, which would give Meredith time to paint and Alan the opportunity to embark on a new writing project that he had been putting off for over a year.

Collin was right when he said Meredith would have lots of potential clients. After his party, she was flooded with requests. She figured she had about six months before the filming started, so she agreed to accept six clients, one per month. It ended up being a great diversion from the day-to-day tasks of laundry, cleaning, and grocery shopping. She quietly disappeared during nap time, emerging completely fulfilled by the time her little angels awoke with bright, happy faces.

"I have some news I think you're going to find very interesting," Alan said mysteriously.

"What is it?" Meredith had a pit in her stomach.

"Turns out they have moved the location of the film."

"Please tell me it's not someplace like Fresno."

"Nope."

"Are you going to tell me, or leave me hanging?"

"I think it's cuter when you're hanging. What's it worth to you?" he said, and kissed her behind the ear.

"Alan."

"Okay, San Francisco."

"Seriously?"

"Yep. How is that for working in our own backyard?"

"I can't tell you how excited I am!" Meredith said, clapping her hands.

"Good, that's the way I like you," he said, and started to peel off her sweater.

"The munchkins probably have another thirty minutes of snooze time," Meredith said in a throaty, come-get-me-now voice.

And with that, they tossed aside their clothes like teenagers on a Saturday night. Meredith started along his chest and with her tongue slowly found her way down.

"You are by far the most intoxicating woman I have ever known, Meredith."

He reciprocated, and they ended their romp supine and well satisfied. Just when they were tempted to have another go at it, they heard the familiar babble of two waking babies from the other room. Laughing, they pulled their clothes on and retrieved the pink-faced duo from their cribs. Poppy was not far behind, and they decided to treat themselves to supper out, at their favorite pizza place down the street. It always reminded Meredith and Alan of their honeymoon, because the crust was thin and the toppings layered the same way as the pizzas in Italy. After a walk to the park, they capped the evening with gelato, and the whole family returned home exhausted and ready to go to bed.

Chapter 56

The studio absolutely loved the final script, making only a few minor alterations. They were set to begin filming in three months, and Meredith was beginning to get nervous.

"You are going to be a natural," Alan said.

"I cannot believe how lucky we are that we can alternate our days on set. Kathryn is going to take the kids on Fridays so we can be there together one day a week."

"Sounds good," Alan said.

Just then the phone rang. It was the woman who handled publicity for the studio, wanting to know if Alan and Meredith would be interested in doing a spread for *Architectural Digest*. Meredith laughed as she looked around at the sea of baby toys and laundry that desperately needed to be folded and returned to its proper place. She told the woman she'd get back to her and ventured outside to tell Alan, who was manning the grill.

"I know what this is about," he said.

"What do you mean?"

"I think Collin might be behind this. He has a friend who is one of the managing editors for a magazine, and I am pretty sure I recall that he said it was *Architectural Digest*. You have generated quite a name for yourself, babe."

"Really?"

"I think we should do it," Alan said nonchalantly.

"Well, if we do, we are going to need to hire someone to come in and get this place in order. After all, those magazines are supposed to be the goal, not the 'before' picture!"

Meredith acted like the house was a mess, but in reality it was a showplace, and everyone was always impressed when they visited for the first time. She was known for her casual style of combining the new with the old and making it worthy of any designer magazine.

Within a few weeks the house was "Meredith perfect," as Alan called it, and the East Coast photographers descended upon Larkspur with a vengeance. The coordinator of the event called it the most impeccably photographable town, with just enough California chic. The editors also loved the fact that Alan and Meredith had the most adorable children, who also did well under the camera's eye. They were confident that the spread would be incredibly successful and were anxious to include Meredith's art, as they felt it added so much to the eclectic feel of the property. They would have to wait to see the final product, but Alan and Meredith were encouraged when they took a quick peek at a few of the day's shots.

Turning in, Meredith and Alan laughed. They could not believe that it was over, and they were so pleased that the children had risen to the occasion under the scrutiny of very demanding expectations. It surely would be a fun memory, and Meredith could not wait to send her parents a copy of the monthly publication, which she fondly recalled seeing on the coffee table at her childhood home.

They had a few weeks to go before their daunting filming schedule dismantled their lives. However, considering their proximity to San Francisco, they counted themselves lucky. The director was known for her efficiency, and they felt confident that she would complete the filming within the three-month schedule that she'd mapped out.

When Meredith entered the unfamiliar world of movie making, she initially stood back and observed. She wanted to contribute but felt like she should get her footing before plunging in. By the second week, she had a good idea of her role and felt a great working connection with the impressive direction of Kate Simmons. The formidable filmmaker was everything Meredith could have hoped for and more. She had great instincts, yet appreciated the input of those around her. Meredith could not get over how inspired she was by the collaborative efforts of the production team. She especially loved working on Fridays, because that was the day she and Alan worked together.

The film wrapped right on schedule. Before they knew it they were toasting with champagne and saying their goodbyes to some of the best up-and-coming actors of the decade.

"This was one of the greatest opportunities, Kate," Meredith said.

"It was my pleasure, Meredith. I hope we can work together again after book number two comes out!"

On the drive home, Alan smiled as Meredith told him about her conversation with Kate. She was on cloud nine and could not get over how fulfilling her career as a writer had become.

"It sounds to me like you'd better get started on book two, babe."

"I guess so," Meredith said with a sigh.

"We have a few months before postproduction begins. Maybe we should rent that house in Stinson Beach for a while. It may give you some added inspiration."

"Oh, Alan, that would be great!"

Within a week they were setting up shop at the beach. Meredith had forgotten how magical it was early in the morning, looking over the ocean and breathing in the marine air. Occasionally, she would walk along the surf before the kids got up, simply giving thanks for everything that she had been blessed with.

She established a regular writing schedule, working before the family rose in the morning and in the middle of the afternoon when everyone went down for a two-hour nap. She figured that it would take a little longer to complete, but she was not in a big rush to finish. After all, finishing only meant publicity, book tours, and time away from the family. Meredith had her priorities straight and always put family first.

Spending two months at the beach was exactly what they needed. The kids loved it, and Meredith and Alan were inspired to nearly complete their respective projects. They knew the film would be resuming soon and felt encouraged that it was going to be a success.

By October the editing was finished, and the film was set to be released on Christmas day. The buzz started early. Much of it surrounded Alan and Meredith, the elusive writing team from Marin County, who had been featured in several magazine articles. They were known for their casual but incredibly chic style, and it did not hurt that their children were equally beautiful. Meredith never took the publicity too seriously and still shied away from the local social climbers who clamored to invite them to their events.

Her second book was almost finished, and she looked forward to a quiet and peaceful Christmas, despite the occasional interview to promote the movie. Christmas day was initially chaotic, though things settled down when the kids started playing with their new toys. They planned to spend the day as a family, even though they'd received several invitations to join other families for holiday festivities. At the end of the day, they received a very happy phone call from Kate Simmons. Alan took the call while Meredith put the babies to bed for a much-needed nap.

"Turns out we have a bit of a success on our hands," Alan said as he hung up the phone.

"That is terrific! I can't believe they know it already, though." Meredith was picking up scraps of wrapping paper from the gifts that peppered the family room floor.

The movie had been the biggest Christmas-day opening of all time, and word on the street was that it was going to be the film to beat come awards season. Of course Alan and Meredith wanted it to be successful, but more importantly, they hoped it would be well respected. And it was! As the weeks passed, it became more and more beloved by the fans and critics. Projections assured audiences that it would be the top contender for the year's best picture.

On an especially foggy January morning their phone rang very early with the news that they had been nominated for an Academy Award. It was surreal to both Alan and Meredith, who were overjoyed. The movie received a total of fourteen nominations, more than any other movie that year. Meredith's phone never stopped ringing. Her friends and family were thrilled and could not believe that she would be attending the Academy Awards as a nominee.

"This is insane," Meredith said to Alan.

"It really is, Meredith. I can't get over it, myself."

The weeks following the nomination were a blur. There were luncheons, interviews, dress fittings, and more publicity than either could have imagined. While Alan had won the coveted award a few years back, the spotlight had been nothing like this, and he credited his terrific partner for the added attention.

As the evening drew near, Alan and Meredith took home two other awards for their impeccable script. They were clearly at the top of their game, and when the envelope was opened at the Oscars, they heard their names yet again. They stared at each other with tears in their eyes. It had been a journey that neither could have expected, and they had done it together.

They approached the stage. Alan was wearing a fantastic tuxedo that fit like a glove, and Meredith took away the breath of everyone in her path. The dress she'd selected was a full-length red sheath that fit her to perfection. They stood before the industry greats and spoke from their hearts, sending love to their children, who were waiting for them at home. Their comments were brief, and the audience was transfixed. Their love story had quickly become legendary, and as they exited the stage the cheers continued. They may have entered the arena as unknowns to those unfamiliar with the film industry, but that evening they were the smashing couple that everyone wanted to read about.

The parties were spectacular, packed with the celebrities Meredith had admired much her life. Alan was more accustomed to the Hollywood scene, so he was less intimidated when engaging in conversation. They sat at a huge table with others from the film and celebrated the ten wins that their movie had taken home until the wee hours of the morning.

"So, Meredith, when am I going to get a look at book number two?" Kate Simmons said from across the table.

"It's nearly complete," Meredith said.

"Well, if it's anything like this one, I think we are going to have another happy marriage."

Alan squeezed Meredith's hand under the table. The couple spent the rest of the evening dancing to the sounds of some of the best musicians of all time.

"I cannot believe we are dancing next to Sting," Meredith whispered to Alan.

He laughed to himself, never tiring of her adorable innocence. Here she just won an Academy Award, and she was mesmerized by those around her.

As soon as they arrived home the next day, golden statue in hand, they looked in on their sleeping children. Vivian, who was never far away from the kids, looked up from her post in the hallway just outside the bedroom doors. Alan and Meredith, beyond exhausted after their whirlwind trip to Los Angeles, flopped immediately into bed.

The days to come were quiet, giving Alan and Meredith a welcome letdown from the two months of Oscar craziness. They rejected any further interviews, as they wanted to resume their private lives in Larkspur. Walks to town and the park were on the daily agenda, and an hour or two in her art studio during nap time was always important to Meredith.

By the end of spring, book number two was completed and submitted for final approval. Spencer had only nominal changes and could not wait to leak a few tidbits to the media. Although this time it would be done in conjunction with the studio so the advertising campaign could be mutually agreed upon before its official release. After the success of the first film, the sequel would certainly be received with great anticipation. Meredith elected not to get involved with the business aspect of it. She was only really interested in the creative process, and she let Alan and their agent handle the logistics of promoting and releasing her latest novel to the public. This time the publicity would be a challenge, as they now had three children in tow. But Alan would be with her for the media tour, which was an enormous relief.

"Well, it appears that my brilliant wife has done it again," Alan said as she descended from her studio happily refreshed.

"What do you mean?"

"I just got off the phone with the agency, and the book is set to be released for the holiday season. Kate has slated the film to go into production a year or so later."

"Fantastic!"

She held the hand of one of the wobbly tots as Poppy proudly took charge of the other. They emerged onto the patio for supper, completely unfazed by their celebrity status. It was yet another combined effort that brought them closer together as a couple, and as a family. Meredith and Alan stood back and watched their three beautiful children play in the afternoon sun, and they knew they had a privileged life. The road had not always been easy, but they always appreciated what they had and greeted every day with love and grace.